Wooing Mr Wickham

Wooing Mr Wickham

Stories inspired by Jane Austen's
Heroes and Villains
Foreword by Michèle Roberts

HONNO MODERN FICTION

First published by Honno
'Ailsa Craig', Heol y Cawl, Dinas Powys,
Wales, CF64 4AH

1 2 3 4 5 6 7 8 9 10

ISBN 978-1-906784-32-4

Published with the financial assistance of the
Welsh Books Council

Cover design: Sue Race, ShedMedia
Text design: G Preston

Printed in Wales by Gomer

CONTENTS

FOREWORD

Jane Austen remains wildly up-to-date. Contemporary critics point out how, for example, she invented the unreliable narrator, and an early form of thriller, in *Emma*, long before anybody else got round to such experiments. The modern idea of writing a story inspired by someone else's characters might have amused that sharp-eyed lady. She liked doing the same kind of thing herself. Steeped in the gothic literary romances of her day, she broke from them, in an astonishing and powerful rupture, to invent something revolutionary: her version of realism. In *Northanger Abbey*, in particular, she both celebrated and mocked the earlier genre and tradition she knew so well. Her heroine Catherine Morland, adrift in contemporary urban life, tries to behave like a heroine of gothic romance, with comic results.

You cannot write well without reading voraciously. Reading writers you admire may make you itch to do something similar yourself. You learn through imitation, until eventually you find a voice, a style, that are your own, and then, as you go on, you find others, and then more again. Who better to begin with, to admire and imitate, than Jane Austen? Each generation reads her afresh, and finds new objects of praise. At the moment, we seem interested in Austen's views on money, on landed property and its inheritance. We also note how slyly she smuggles in details of the world beyond the parsonage windows: war, slavery and other forms of brutality press up against the curtains. At the same time, inside the drawing room we hear the narrator speak about children with a scorn that can amount to cruelty. For modern readers these subjects often come to the fore.

Austen also compellingly describes the sexual double standard of her day, which had its own share of brutality: women socially ruined by having flings, men getting away with it, just about. The main plot in each novel is the marriage plot, as it had to be for the middle-class women of the day, hence the stress on female propriety, that's to say female virginity. A rich hero like Darcy needs to know that his sons are his, in order to pass on his property to them. Outside the house of marriage, however, in each of Austen's novels, lurk all the seduced girls and their illegitimate babies, the sexy, rebellious girls who want adventures, the exploited widows. Their stories come to us filtered by others' voices.

Almost invisible inside the house are the servants. Anne in *Persuasion* recognises that Nurse Rook, midwife to the wealthy ladies of Bath, must have many good stories to tell, gleaned from nipping in and out of so many bedrooms, but she gives these a sentimental gloss. She cannot imagine what Nurse Rook's life is really like, but we can. We can try to, anyway. Nowadays, Nurse Rook tells her own story.

All the stories in this collection recognise that Austen's plots, ending at the closed front door of the house of marriage, the closed bedroom door, can begin again and again. The door swings open. The lid comes off. The writers of these stories have not scrupled to turn Austen's originals inside out, toss them topsy-turvy, tear them apart and collage them, poke holes in them, in order to make something new with them. This kind of writerly aggression is necessary, as Austen herself recognised. The very best of these stories provoke us to admiration and delight, a sense of the absolute rightness of what we read. Congratulations to all the writers in this collection. I enjoyed their work a great deal.

Michèle Roberts
London, July 2011

The Jane Austen Short Story Award was initiated by Chawton House Library to encourage contemporary creative writing. The 2011 competition attracted entries from fifteen countries worldwide, from places as far apart as Serbia and Singapore, Austria and Australia – demonstrating the ever-growing appeal of Austen, both as an author and a source of inspiration.

2011 marks the bicentenary of the publication of *Sense and Sensibility*, the first of the novels to appear in print. Chawton House – the former home of Jane's brother Edward – is reminiscent of Delaford, the 'nice old-fashioned place full of comforts and conveniences' owned by Colonel Brandon. Edward Austen Knight inherited the Manor of Chawton after being adopted by wealthy, childless relatives and offered his sister a new home on his estate. Her arrival in the Hampshire village marked the start of what was to be the most productive period of her literary life. *Sense and Sensibility*, *Pride and Prejudice*, *Emma* and *Mansfield Park* were all published while she lived in the village. *Northanger Abbey* and *Persuasion* were published posthumously after her death at the age of just 41.

So the Great House, as Edward's Elizabethan mansion was known then, was inextricably linked with Jane Austen's destiny. It was recently saved from ruin by an American philanthropist who is a devoted Austen fan. For centuries it was the comfortable country home of the Knight family but following the First World War it fell into decline due to inheritance taxes and ever-increasing running costs – the fate of many other country estates in England. By 1987, when Richard Knight inherited the property from his father, it was on the verge of financial and physical collapse. Its associations with Jane Austen looked destined to become mere memories.

Sandy Lerner, co-founder of Cisco Systems, Inc., learnt of this misfortune and decided that Chawton House could be the perfect home for her collection of books by the long-forgotten early English women writers who were Austen's literary mothers and sisters. In Sandy's vision, Chawton House would be the ideal environment for research and study in a manner that would bring to life the social, domestic, economic, cultural and historical context in which the writers lived and worked. In short, a unique opportunity to study the works in an appropriate setting.

She acquired a long lease on the house and began an extensive programme of conservation work. It re-opened in 2003 as Chawton House Library – the world's first centre for the study of the lives and works of women writing in English before 1830. As well as an original manuscript and early editions of Jane Austen's work, authors such as Mary Shelley, Mary Wollstonecraft, Frances Burney and Aphra Behn feature in the collection of more than 8,000 books. The library is open by appointment to members of the public and there are visiting fellowships available for more specialised research.

It is to be hoped that, two centuries on, Austen will continue to inspire a new generation of writers.

Lindsay Ashford, July 2011

For more information about Chawton House Library, visit the website: www.chawtonhouse.org

ANNIE'S SECOND CHANCE

Mary Fitzpatrick

Annie's Second Chance

꒰Ꙇ

Mary Fitzpatrick

When I was a kid the thing I loved best in the world was to be allowed into Aunt Annie's bedroom. It happened most often on a Friday evening, just after she got in from working at the bakery, before we were called downstairs for our fish and chips. It was a weekly ritual, really, pretending I was taking in *Romper Room* on the telly while all the time I was listening to her wearily mount the stairs. On hearing her door close I'd creep up after her, carefully avoiding the creaky tread halfway up, as if I were a burglar up to no good and afraid of being caught. Then I'd stand at the top, listening to the minute rustles and clatters as she changed her clothes and kicked off her working shoes, the sharp rattle as she laid her watch and earrings on the dressing table and, finally, the muffled sigh and small 'boing' of springs as she sat down on the bed.

Moving towards her door I'd place one large, pinkish ear against the wood; at that moment, as if she could sense me hovering, Annie would always call out, "Col? Is that you son? Come on in and tell me about yer day." Inside the room was filled with her scent – freshly baked bread, tobacco, faded lavender, sweat. She'd usually be lying back on the bed, rubbing her stockinged toes or scratching her head through its frizzy red curls, stretching and smoking. Through a blue fug she'd say, "Well?" – her invitation for me to sit on the end of the bed and talk...

"Mikey Shanley told me I was fat today, Aunt Annie."

Annie pulled her long, lantern-jawed face into a scowl. "Shanley, that wee skelf? He needs a good feed, that one. Jist you tell him from me that my Col is going to be a looker, that Hollywood'll be beatin a path to his door..." Trailing off she took another long, deep drag from her fag before pointing at me and shaking her head. "That boy'd no doubt call Rock Hudson fat just 'cause he's a fine big fella, *unlike* Mr Shanley..."

Knowing that this monologue could go on for a while, I got on with what I'd really come into Annie's room for, and that was to have a look at her "outfits". Gently easing myself off the bed I sidled towards the wardrobe and, before gingerly opening up, glanced over my shoulder; she was still lying back, her arm over her eyes, the ash from her cigarette long and dangling. I saw that she was sleepy so I slowly pulled back the doors and put out my hands to touch the marvels within: the midnight blue grosgrain silk gown she'd worn to last year's Bakery Ball in Dublin, the one with the fishtail, spaghetti straps and little diamanté clips; the mustard yellow sateen swing coat, always teamed with her red snakeskin shoes and matching bag; the dusky pink linen suit, with the chevron tucks at the front and cloth covered buttons on the back... I touched them tenderly, the evening wear and the day clothes, the velvet and the tweed, the tartan and satin, all giving off the scent of moth balls and *4711 Cologne*. Within me something stirred, a little worm of desire that started in my stomach and spread to my loins.

Then I stood on tiptoe, bringing my eyes level with the top shelf where the hats sat. Pillbox, berets, knitted pixies, pom-poms, tassels, veils and waxen cherries all jostling for attention. And right at the back was the prize, the black and white straw number the size of a cartwheel, the one I'd never seen her wearing, apart from in a little black and white photo which she kept in a green leather-bound album. This was taken by a street photographer because, she claimed, she'd been "the spit of Rita Hayworth" in her younger days. I presumed that he, like me, wore milk bottle specs. The man standing next to her sported a chalk-stripe suit and a rather sweet smile; I liked his face, his high cheekbones and fair, crinkly hair, the large eyes that I could tell were a bright, piercing blue, even in black and white.

On Saturday mornings I always brought her in a tray with tea and toast and sat on her dressing table chair while she surfaced. She kept the green photo album propped up against the mirror and, as she coughed and sniffed awake, I'd flick through it, always pausing at the one of her and the mystery man. I was drawn to it but, for some reason that I couldn't put my finger on, I was wary of asking questions.

One morning she caught me frowning over it; gesturing towards me with a piece of toast she asked, "What've ye discovered, son?"

I carried the album over to the bed and pointed shyly towards the picture. "Who *is* he?"

Annie swung her long, skinny legs out of the bed and pulled the album onto her knee; rubbing the surface of the photo she carefully smoothed out its curling edges. "Oh, that's Frank Weaver, Col, an old flame. Long gone, son, long gone."

"What happened to him?"

She stood up and moved towards the window. "Well, Col, he wanted me to marry him but it never worked out. At least..." she trailed off and turned back towards me, her face chalk white. "...Yer granddad didn't like him, ye see."

"Why?"

She reached for her green Chinese silk dressing gown and shrugged into it. "Because Frank decided to go to England and join the army and yer granddad hated the English with a vengeance. He said that if I had anything to do with Frank I'd better never come back into this house."

My mammy and I had moved in with Granddad and Aunt Annie when I was a baby, after my dad had been knocked down by a lorry outside Barry's The Bookie. As a teenager I could hardly remember Granddad, he'd died when I was only four, but I could still smell his breath, a strange melange of rotten teeth and the mints which he seemed to have perpetually on the go. I could also still see his round head, bald and blank as a billiard ball.

Annie gave a little grunt and looked out of the window. "Even though yer granddad was dead set against us I was prepared to just run away with Frank but yer mammy, well, she talked me out of it, convinced me that Frank was no good, that I was giving up too much." She laid her forehead against the glass and I could imagine what she was seeing; the scrubby front garden with the dying privet hedge catching the litter of bus tickets and sweetie papers which flew down our narrow little street on what seemed to be a constantly bitter wind. "This – *this* – is what I'd have been giving up, this little paradise." She wrapped her arms around herself, her shoulders shaking. When I told Mammy that Aunt Annie seemed upset she just 'tsked' and carried on vigorously polishing the fire brasses, her round, red face almost as shiny as the metal.

A few weeks before my fourteenth birthday Annie came in after work and sat at the kitchen table; it was a Friday and I was expecting her to go up to her room as usual but she seemed intent on lingering, picking at the corner of her freshly painted thumbnail (Revlon's 'Cherries in the Snow'; I'd seen her applying it the night before, her tongue thrust out in concentration as she made each careful, silken stroke). Mammy was at the sink, cutting chips while I sat at the other end of the table from Annie, studying my maths homework, ears pricked for whatever news was about to be spilled.

"Don't bother with tea for me tonight, Tessie. I'm going out."

Mammy glanced over her shoulder, the small, sharp knife that she used to cut the chips poised in mid-air. "Well, well, got a date, have ye?" Her eyes had narrowed but they were also alight with mischief.

"Yes, as a matter of fact I have." Annie averted her eyes and toyed with a few grains of sugar, chasing them round the yellow Formica-topped table. "Ye'll never guess who it is."

Mammy wiped her hands on her pinny and came towards the table. "It's that big TJ Elliott, no doubt. He's been after ye for long enough." TJ Elliott was the local butcher, a man with a blood stained apron which turned my stomach every time I had to run the messages for Mammy. He was a widower and, although it was acknowledged that he was quite a catch, it was also rumoured that he'd bullied and beaten his wife for years before she'd given up the ghost. It was also whispered that he'd 'done' his former business partner, Charlie Smethurst, who'd gone back to Dublin and died a penniless alcoholic.

Annie continued to gaze at the top of the table, her slender fingers rubbing the grains of sugar back and forth, back and forth. "No, it's not him." Now she looked up, her treacle-coloured eyes round and intense. "It's Frank, Tessie, Frank Weaver. He came into the bakery the other day to buy half a dozen rolls for his auld mammy. I didn't know where to look but I think he was even more flabbergasted than me, his face went pure scarlet." The words were now coming out in a rush while my eyes darted between my suddenly animated aunt and my mother, who was now grim faced and chewing the inside of her mouth.

"What? Frank Weaver after all these years? What's brought

him back to Clondalkin? Are the *English* not good enough for him, now?"

When I recently told this story to my young Swedish lover, Eric, he pursed his lips and I could see that he was trying not to laugh. To someone like him, who came out to his parents when he was *twelve*, for God's sake, the idea of someone having to seek permission to love is frankly ludicrous. But the past, as they say, is a different country, they do things differently there – especially in southern Ireland in 1963.

"Oh, for God's sake, Tessie, half of this country lives in Liverpool or Birmingham or Glasgow. What the hell is there here for us – for *me* - now?" Annie had straightened up in her chair and, for the first time, I noticed a steeliness in her smoky voice.

Mammy pressed the point of the knife into the surface of the table, her own voice quivering as she said, "There's yer family for one thing, madam. And just think what black burning shame it would have brought on us if ye'd married a British soldier."

Annie jumped up, nearly toppling her chair. "Aw, Jesus, Tess, you're not going to start all that again, are ye? That auld story about Grandpa Craven?"

Family myth-making had it that Grandpa Craven had been dragged out into a ditch in Connemara and shot by a drunken Black and Tan shortly after the Easter uprising; this fact was never verified as a body was never found. Another branch of the family, less loyal to the legend, had it that he'd done a bunk to the States, leaving behind a wife and ten children.

"That's not the point," Mammy continued, "because if I've said it once I've said it a hundred times, that man Weaver has nothing to offer ye, Annie, nothing."

"Oh, aye, ye'd have me go with that TJ Elliot, wouldn't ye, even though everyone knows he's a rotter." Annie had run out of the

14

kitchen door and was now halfway up the stairs.

Mammy stood at the bottom and shouted, "Well, ye needn't think Frank Weaver'll darken my door." Turning round she found me at her back. "And what are you gawking at, ya eejit? Lay the table, for mercy's sake."

Things were pretty icy round the house after that; Annie continued to see Frank Weaver and Mammy 'hmphed' every time she passed her in the hall. Then one night, about a fortnight later, Mammy walked into my room without knocking. I was lying on top of the bed in my underpants reading *Madame Bovary*; she eyed the novel suspiciously but luckily I'd wrapped it in a cover taken from Thomas à Kempis' *Counsels on the Spiritual Life*. I sat up and insouciantly placed Emma into my bedside drawer.

"Do you know anything about this?" Mammy started without preamble.

"About what?"

She rolled her eyes. "About Frank Weaver having a *Good Job*."

A Good Job was anything that was done indoors, where you wore a suit and tie and which, at the end of the day, carried a pension.

"No, she never said."

Mammy rolled her eyes again, indicating that I was both an eejit and a galoot. "I've just been talking to Bridie McCann; turns out Frank Weaver's only over here for a few weeks, his auld mammy's got the shingles. Turns out he's a surveyor of some sort, high up in the profession, overseeing other fellas. In London." This last added a final golden sheen to the new revelation; you might hate the English but London was El Dorado, beyond the pettiness of nation and race.

The next night Mammy brought home a steak pie made by TJ Elliott himself while Annie provided the half dozen cream cakes, in a white box tied up with a red and blue ribbon. Everything indicated that it was going to be a special occasion. At half past six a soft knock sounded on the rarely used front door. Both Annie and Mammy stood at the same time but Mammy got there first, pulling off her pinny as she went while Annie primped her ginger hair. Out in the hall we heard Mammy say, "Frank, it's lovely to see ye again, what a long time it's been. Come right in, ye're a sight for sore eyes."

The date for Frank and Annie's wedding was set for the autumn. I, of course, helped her pick her outfit. I voted for ivory slipper silk but she laughed and shook her head. "No, I don't think so, son, that wouldn't be right." Eventually we settled on a soft woollen suit in a blue green shade which, we were informed, was called Marina. On the bus back home we nestled up close on the back seat; as it turned into our street she took my hand in hers and said, "Col, just remember one thing, always listen to your gut and then follow your heart. And never, ever let anyone persuade ye otherwise."

My inspiration: The inspiration for this story is taken from *Persuasion*. I feel that the story of Anne Elliot and Captain Wentworth has a universality to it, that it could still occur at any time, in any place. People give misguided advice and the receiver of the advice often feels, for whatever reason, obliged to take it.

HENRY TILNEY ATTEMPTS TO CURE HIS WIFE

Sarah Taylor

Henry Tilney Attempts to Cure his Wife

꙰

Sarah Taylor

The morning that he found his wife with her ear to the floorboards in one of the guest bedrooms, Henry Tilney knew that she was "back on the novels again". The house had been pleasantly free from such adventures for some time, save for a minor relapse over the Brontës just before Easter, which thankfully had passed without anything too calamitous. It was true that Catherine had taken longer walks than usual in the hills around the parsonage swathed in any woollen shawls she could lay her hands upon, but there had been little to suggest that she was falling back into her old ways, save for one incident at breakfast when she was halfway through *Jane Eyre*. On that morning Henry had caught Catherine staring at him and, on asking her whether anything was wrong, she had told him that he was "deplorably cheerful", and asked why he couldn't be a little more brooding. Puzzling over this odd request he had frowned deeply at her, with the result that she was far happier for the rest of the day. He had arranged for a servant to lose *Jane Eyre* as soon as she could be located in the house.

He knew that Catherine could not help herself, and her curiously intense approach to books was part of what had charmed him about her in the first place, but on the whole he was happier when

Catherine was involved in something other than reading. She had proved as good a wife to him as he had been a husband to her, which was to say excellent, and they were very happy together. He knew, though, that he could not keep her forever occupied with parish works, or the children, or busy her with tasks to do in the parsonage, and the temptation for her to find fresh mischief in the library was ever present.

The first year of their marriage had been the most troublesome. After he had weaned her off the gothic romances that had helped bring them together, she had discovered the even darker horrors lurking in a story of vampirism recommended by a friend. "It must be shockingly good, Henry," she announced over tea while the children tripped round the lawn pretending to bite one another. "It is by a friend of Lord Byron." As ever with Catherine, reading one book led to another, and within weeks she was locking all windows at night and Henry was thoroughly sick of the smell of garlic.

Together they had weathered the storms of romance, horror and comedy, but in general Catherine's break-outs had caused little consternation. Henry had put up with her taking the children fairy-hunting in the gardens, seeing endless ghosts in the kitchens late at night and desperately trying to matchmake the young folk of the parish. He had not minded too much when, ten years into their marriage, she had taken to peering up into the belltower instead of attending to his sermon, convinced that some poor deformed creature might be taking refuge there. Nor had he cared that, a decade later, she referred to every plain child baptised in the church as "a swan in the making". There had been some rather more difficult incidents, however. Everyone agreed that it had been most unfortunate that her reading *Frankenstein* came so soon after the death of the children's favourite kitten.

Such behaviour had, however, been less prevalent of late, so it was a shock to find Catherine lying on the bedroom floor, her ear pressed close to the floorboards.

"Do we have mice, dearest?" Henry asked.

Catherine looked up at him, her face a mask of horror.

"I think I can hear heartbeats, Henry," she whispered.

Henry frowned. He suspected the volume of Poe, which he had found in her needlecase that morning. Catherine always had known where to hide her reading.

"Nothing of the sort, Catherine, I'm sure," he said. He hoped he sounded firm. It was the tone of voice he reserved for when the Parish Council was being particularly difficult over some little aspect of the running of the church. His wife followed their lead and ignored him.

"I feel sure it is a warning, Henry," she said. "Some dreadful secret that will unmask us both."

Henry sighed deeply. This was a bad relapse. He wondered whether he should bring out the volume of poetry that he had been keeping for just such an occasion as this. Something soothing and rural to settle Catherine's nerves. Surely there could be no harm in that. He had checked in advance to see that there were no influences of Lord Byron in it. There was nothing much else in the library that would seem suitable. Catherine had no taste for history and he had given up trying to get her to read theology several years ago. Not because she showed no interest in it, but because theology went the way of all her other reading. She became too immersed in it, too caught up in the moment of it, too keen to get involved in it all. It was very embarrassing to have one's wife interrupt one's sermons.

When Catherine entered the library later that night she found that the entire Poe section had gone. She frowned. It was most tiresome of Henry to overreact like this. She still had her suspicions concerning *Jane Eyre. She* had not lost the book, of that she was sure, and she had been so close to finding out Mr Rochester's secret. Did Henry have any secrets, she wondered? It would have thrilled her to the bone to think that he did, but he was so depressingly prosaic. It was no use imagining that he was gone from the house too long because he was visiting a secret lover or engaged in underhand dealings with a band of swarthy smugglers, when she knew full well that any delay to his arrival at the dinner table was down to nothing more nor less than a sick parishioner or two.

She was just wondering whether to give history another try when one of the maids staggered in, bowed almost double under a weight of books, which she dropped to the floor in a manner of intense irritation. Seeing Catherine, she dropped a swift curtsey and began to gather them into a neat pile.

"Begging your pardon, m'am," the girl said. "These are newly arrived from Mr Simpson, and the master distinctly said that they should be in place tonight." The girl picked up a stray volume that had fallen near the library's great oak desk, and as she did so a slim magazine fell from between its pages. Sensing mystery (she did little else since the disappearance of *Jane Eyre*), Catherine darted forward and snatched it up from the floor.

"*English Women's Journal*?" she mused aloud. "Not a publication I have heard of. I'll take this one, Ellis. Carry on with the rest." She went to find a quiet spot in which to read.

The next day at breakfast, Catherine was attacking her egg with great purpose when Henry came in, unaware of the tirade that lay in wait for him. He had just settled down with a plate of kedgeree when his wife laid down her spoon and, fixing him with a very hard stare, made her announcement.

"Henry, dear, I don't wish to upset you, but I think I'm being oppressed."

Henry swallowed a mouthful of fish and looked at her placidly.

"Really Catherine, by whom?"

Catherine gave it some thought. "Well partly by you, I think, but the general edifice of England's political system is also responsible."

"Is it really?"

"Yes. You are but part of a machine that keeps women very firmly in their place and stops them from reaching their full potential. I'm sure you can't help it, though." She smiled encouragingly at him.

This was rather new. Henry had never considered himself to be the oppressive type. He had had far too much of his father's heavy-handedness to wish that on his own wife and children. However, dear Catherine was most certainly in earnest, and he tried to frame a conciliatory reply.

"I shall try to reform, Catherine, if that is what you wish."

"Oh, my dear," she said, "it is not you I wish to reform. It is society. We must rise against our oppressors. I wonder if I could stand for Parliament."

She reached for another slice of toast.

A miserable few weeks followed for Henry Tilney. Spurred on by the writers of essays on industrial employment, intellectual freedom and the reform of a vast range of laws, which she insisted were "insidious to right thinking" while refusing to darn his socks, Catherine took to schooling the maids in the principles of female emancipation. Although she took Henry to task regularly on the lot of women in the Bible, she did not revert to interrupting his sermons. Instead, she would loudly interject "...and womankind" at any point in the service where God's relationship to "mankind" was mentioned. This created quite a stir and, when he could bear it no longer, Henry resorted to the mean trick of bribing his eldest child to distract her at the crucial moments so as to enable morning worship to pass in peace.

One afternoon, while they were out in the garden together, Catherine informed Henry that she would be using the church hall for an hour or so.

"Of course, my dear," said Henry. "A ladies meeting?"

"Yes," said Catherine, dead-heading a rose. "Female suffrage. A worthy cause. I have been reading up about it. I have called a public meeting." She left the house, waving her hands at an imaginary audience and muttering under her breath about "sisters long oppressed by inequality" and "the rights of Eve".

Henry sat up late, waiting for her return. When she had not come back by ten in the evening he set out for the village. He found Catherine sitting forlorn in an empty hall, the benches in neat rows with pamphlets entitled *The New Womanliness* atop each one. Henry's heart sank. He could not bear that Catherine be disappointed. He crossed to the front of the hall, sat down, and motioned for her to begin her speech.

Catherine stood up. "No, Henry, I don't think they were ready. Not everyone has sufficient imagination for change. Let us go home."

In the days that followed this disaster Henry racked his brain as to how to cheer Catherine up. He invited their friends round to weekend parties, took her on outings, and bought her yard after yard of pretty muslin, but all to no effect. She remained downcast and depressed. It was when he was in the village stationers ordering a new Parish Register that Henry Tilney had his brainwave. He had always known Catherine to have imagination. He had never known anyone who could bring a book, an idea, a belief, to life as she could. If her reading was constantly leading her into trouble, why should he not try her on the pen instead? He purchased a notebook, large and square with good crisp sheets and a binding that would put up with much creasing, and presented Catherine with it over breakfast. For a while he believed her to be happier. She avoided the library and could be seen, bent low over the book, sat under the apple tree in the garden for hours at an end. Henry busied himself with his parish work and left her to herself, content that he had found an end to all their troubles.

For a few weeks they lived very contentedly together. Then one sunny morning in April, Henry found Catherine in her usual place under the apple tree, her head in her hands, crying. The notebook lay beside her. Henry dropped to his knees and took his wife's hands in his.

"What on earth is the matter, Catherine?"

She made no reply but only howled all the louder and motioned towards the notebook. Henry picked it up and flicked through the pages.

"Dearest, this is empty."

Catherine sniffed and raised her head to look at him.

"Oh Henry, I'm so ashamed! I can't do it. I just can't write. I've tried and tried, but nothing comes out. I'm not sure I want it to. Henry, this isn't what I want to do at all!"

Henry was taken aback.

"Nonsense Catherine, your imagination has always been... Well I can't say it's always been easy to live with, but I cannot deny that you have a most wonderful talent."

Catherine shook her head.

"I don't want to create other worlds. My genius, if you can call it that, for all the trouble it's caused you, is in living fully in the worlds of others, the ideas of others. I don't just consume a book, Henry, I inhabit it. I give it the dignity of being everything it is meant to be. I have lived great lives. I have been Catherine on that moor, and Jane creeping through the night with her candle. I have been a living poem, and most of all I have played out to other women what a woman can be when she believes in things. I have lived a life of freedom and potential, and one day others will too. I know the meeting was a failure, but one day women will catch sight of a new world shown to them through the imagination of another, and when they see that new world, they will reach out and grasp it so tight that no one will wrest it from them. I think that is my talent, Henry. I wasn't born to write books. I was born to let them write me, to let their worlds and ideas live fully *through* me. Don't they deserve that? The truly great ones? The ones that matter? The ones that will change our world?"

Henry looked at his wife's tear-stained face. He knew that what he planned to do next would probably mean that Catherine would spend the next two weeks skulking round the attic rooms looking for hidden doorways, or lecturing their jolly housemaids on their unhappy lot, but he could not fight against her nature any longer. Nor was he sure that he wanted to. He picked up the notebook, patted Catherine on the hand and set off for the house. Someone must be sent to town to purchase a fresh copy of *Jane Eyre*.

❦

My inspiration: I love how Catherine Morland so fully inhabits the books she reads. I wondered what effect this would have on domestic life – and what would happen if she encountered any truly radical writings.

THE LOVE OBJECT

Deirdre Shanahan

The Love Object

ঽৄ

Deirdre Shanahan

He doesn't see me and can't tell how I feel, and tonight when he lies down he will not think of me or the others – though maybe he will and maybe we do mean more to him than just a bunch of teenagers he has to look after.

We are kids who cannot clean potatoes, so he shows us; peel coiling off like clothes falling, creamy and thick, his fingers entwined. He cuts chunky sticks and throws them into the pan of fat where bubbles gallop and spring. It is evening and he has won us over, hands down, by letting us play music while Clemmie lays the table because she's not so clumsy. We gather around while steam rises from the potatoes and his steel-grey eyes soften.

Gerard says he will buy brushes and paint the walls, but when it comes to it the lads aren't interested, though I am and would paint every wall in the house with him. What does he do in his free time, when he must be glad to be shot of us? Hayley, who is tall and leggy and keeps overdosing, Clemmie who keeps running off to her uncle's, plus Steven and others who show up for short stays.

In the visiting room, with the sound down on the TV, I can read my magazines. It wouldn't be so bad if there was someone to talk to but everyone comes with their suitcase of problems. They act big in the hope that they will get chucked out or moved on to another place. They think they will have their own room and bigger televisions. It's not worth it, because I've been elsewhere and this place, nevermind the shitty carpets and the bulging sofas, has central heating. A person can start to feel looked after in warmth.

"Aelish? You should be at school," Anna calls. "Didn't Gerard call you? Why didn't you go?"

"Didn't fancy it."

"I didn't fancy school but I had to go there," she says.

Yeah and look where it got you, I dare not say. She flicks through files. A shabby pink one falls out.

"Turnham High..." she says.

"I don't care."

"I can take you in the car."

No one is going to take me to school. Upstairs in the room, I lie down. God this place stinks. Shit and detergent, cigarettes and drink. No one ever cleans it. Steven is lucky. Soon he'll be home. His parents want him back. My mum says she's had enough, and my dad went off years ago. I don't mind. It's got the freedom, the pool table, the meals and Gerard with his bit of an accent, from the north like my dad. It folds around you. He's too nice for this place and I can't work out why he stays. He studied up there then came south.

He tells me he went walking as a student, over the hills and moors. It sounds crazy; all that bad weather. He walked miles into hours and shows me pictures. He wears a shirt with a hood. It's dark blue and if it wasn't so obviously his, I'd say me and it had a future. When it's warm, he takes it off and drapes it over a chair in long, deep folds, pockets of a downy inside. If I let myself, I could wear it.

Anna opens the door and doesn't see me at first.

"Aelish McKerrow. Shift yourself."

"I'm not going. That school never did anything for me."

"I didn't say you were. I've just had a call from your social worker. She wants to see you."

"Tell her I'm out."

"I can't," Anna says.

"Why not?"

"Because you're here."

I grab my jacket. I don't want a social worker poking her nose into my business. I've no reason to see her. I've done nothing wrong.

I go by the canal where I came with Hayley. The water is gungy. She said she had seen swans here and there were locks further up. She said she'd like to live on a boat. I said, it's not so bad at number thirty-nine, but she said it made her feel pent up and mad and she'd have more room on a little boat.

"I'm gonna get out. Just watch," she says pulling her jacket close.

I thought she was screwy then. Nice but screwed up.

Outside HMV, she's loud and full of herself, thinking she's big, because of the knife she carries.

"Going in?" I ask.

"Been there. Look." She opens her hand to reveal a slide of three CDs. "Nice, isn't it?"

"Now where?" Steven asks, poking his fingers right down the deep pocket of a long, black, coat.

"The arcade? I want to get more stuff."

"You can't. You won't be able to hold everything."

"I said I was doing work experience." Hayley laughs, her yellowy teeth showing.

*

We all go to the park and smoke. Hayley says she has found out about a party and will get a lift from someone she met in a pub. Her face is smooth with pleasure. Clemmie drifts ahead, kicking a stone. She was always better at listening.

"Gerard might be there," she adds. "It's supposed to be a party by someone who works in Grange House, you know the place for really cracked-up adults."

"Will he?" Steven adds.

"Yeah." Her lips smack down. So that was how it was.

"What do you think of Gerard?" she asks.

"He's all right," I say.

"You like him?"

"Better than Anna, who's like she's had a charisma by-pass."

She laughs, lashes snapping fast, her eyes hard.

"I might get off with him," she says.

I wanted to claw her, spoil her bitchy face so that no one'd take any notice of her at the party.

"I thought you didn't like him," Clemmie says.

"It'd be a laugh." Hayley cackles a hideous laugh.

How could she think like that? He told me about things; I know more about him. I couldn't bear to be with her, but she goes off to nick a dress. I go around the shops but can't think straight so I don't take anything. Hayley has smudged the day. I say we should go to the pub. We drink cider, then lager, then shorts. I feel sick.

"We'll have to climb over the wall and go in the back," Clemmie says.

"You'll have to heave me up. I can just about stand."

Somehow we get down the road. Clemmie holds my arm.

We make a noise going in the back door and Anna appears in her old red dressing gown which is like a bedspread. She says Gerard'll speak to us in the morning, making us feel like a couple of kids.

She tells him about us, the bitch. I feel stupid hearing him go on about reports and safety. I try to say to him it was a mistake and anyway how was the party? Did he see Hayley?

"What are you talking about?" he asks.

"She was at that party last night. You must have seen her." I go on.

"I wasn't at any party. Anyway I'm not discussing her."

When we have tea, over the salmon sandwiches, Steven tells me that Hayley is sick. I don't want Gerard to think I'm as stupid as her, so I come down later in my nightdress. The door of the office is ajar and the fluorescent light is on. I tap lightly and inside he is in the blue jacket, I suppose because it's chilly and the fire doesn't work properly. He looks nice with his thick hair all standing up.

"Aelish. What do you want?" Gerard asks.

If I could make him like me more. If I could...

"You'd better go back and tell me whatever it is in the morning. I'm sure it can wait," he says.

But it can't. I want him to know... I'm sorry I came in late... I know I'm younger than him...

"I'd rather—" I begin.

"Wait till morning. It's too cold for you to be hanging around at gone eleven, and I've got some stuff to write up."

He throws me out. That's what it feels like in the dead of night when it's quiet and there's no one about and the landing lights are off. The floor is cold under my feet and my long tee-shirt flaps.

Hayley gets better and no more is said. Gerard cooks, makes us wash up in turn, continues to sort out quarrels about the television and tidies up. He leaves his jacket around. I would like to try it on but decide I had better not, in case he should see me. The next day when he's off duty, it hangs on the back of a chair. I want nothing else. It fits. Suits me nicely. It will do for trips out. I take it and Gerard doesn't notice. I shove it behind a cushion. That's why I can't believe it when I see the blue jacket lying in Hayley's drawer, the way you would stash away a packet of biscuits, or condoms, a magazine or a nice pair of tights. I sweep my hand along soft blue folds, gathering it. She's not getting away with that.

Hayley is in the doorway when I come out of the bedroom.

"What's that?" she asks.

"Nothing."

"Funny kind of nothing. What've you got?"

She goes for me and we fall on the floor, her arms flying. She pulls, kicks me and I punch her. It was his but now it's mine. I push her and she is face down, whining. I pound her. I get up on her back and pull her hair. She squeals like a mouse on fire. I hate her. Burn. Burn. You won't get this. She wriggles away. Her thighs are fat and heavy. Stumpy thick muscles in her calves quiver, they're fish skimming a river. You'll never walk again after I've finished. She is on the bed doubled up. I get her in the stomach. She cries when I leave. Good.

She doesn't say anything later and no one else does. No one would have heard anyway, most of the kids are out, if not at school then around the shops. Pale, ill-looking, she slopes around. People will think it's over a bloke and that it doesn't matter. Even Gerard doesn't take much notice. But he's hardly in the house.

Next day we hear he's leaving. Anna says he's got promoted and is taking over another home, which has been without a manager. I'm shocked. Blasted out of myself. How can he do that? Walk off. I don't know what to do with myself. He belongs here. He can't have any other life.

What will become of us? Will things go on, like they used to? I still have his jacket. I know because I check. It lies the way I folded it. Hayley is going to Ramsgate House, a long-term place where she can't keep going off. Clemmie says the way Hayley kept breaking up her mum's place doesn't help and there's nowhere else that can take her.

I don't see her go. She gathers her stuff and is off. I go down town with Clemmie and two new girls and take them to the fish shop and the bloke with flowers tattooed on his arms dunks his hands among slabs of ice. Petals swim and scales run. He dips and delves, wears an earring and a woolly cap. I don't suppose he's as clever as Gerard. He's not as good-looking.

I don't believe it until I see the papers. Hayley was found in the canal, after taking a load of drugs. She was hardly visible except for the blue jacket, with all the crap and rubbish thrown in. They took her to hospital and expect she'll revive. I read to Clemmie as she can't read. She leans forward in the chair. I could tell her anything and she would believe it.

I rush out to the canal, going down the alley and there's a bare, useless part of ground that isn't even allotments but has a mattress and loads of TVs in the grass. The water is a dark, seeping strand. I see Hayley fall, her hands grasping, water drawing her, lap, lap, lapping, loving. Little waves crawl and jump, push against the blue jacket. I wanted it, to wrap around my body, but instead she's got it. Got him.

Gerard has gone. He has been away for a month but I keep thinking he'll slip back to deliver a report, see someone for a meeting, or see us, but he never comes and never will. Memories rush. He drowns in my heart.

My inspiration: Pride and Prejudice. I have noted and been influenced by the portrayal of relationships which Jane Austen creates; the anxious rivalries over small and important matters – for example the contrast between Elizabeth and Miss Bingley – in a contained world.

THE PLEASURES OF THE OTHER

Paul Brownsey

The Pleasures of the Other

❧

Paul Brownsey

She is entirely unattractive, the servant who opens the door to him beneath the fantastical Gothic porch that calls up to the imagination *Udolpho*-like horrors: an incarcerated female, unspeakable villainy, fiendish ordeals. It calls them up all too fittingly.

That he can size up this woman's charms reassures him: it shows he's not at all intimidated by the difficult interview ahead. The face is as thin as a curse, lips recall a pig's snout, one eye squints somewhere to his right. Altogether, it's a face sufficiently witch-like for one of those tall black steeple-hats they wear here in Wales. What instead covers her hair, completely, is something like a nun's white wimple. The association of ideas with M Diderot's *The Nun* reminds him to look more carefully at her, for signs of certain passions, but not even the thought of those passions spreads upon her the power to evoke desire. What he takes to be a Welsh accent is barely penetrable; she seems to say that the ladies will see him directly.

Is this the chapel he is shown into? Books abound, so presumably it isn't. But it displays the same fancy as the porch outside. Panelling and furniture are carved into Gothic shapes, the rioting foliage of the cornice could strangle a man, a chair is canopied like a bishop's in a cathedral. There is a heavy scent of musk, a Gothic incense.

The three pointed stone arches of the windows turn the lawns and shrubbery beyond into a nunnery garden. Well, it is widely known that this is no place for the male sex. And here are the celebrated – no, notorious – Ladies of Llangollen, at either end of what might be a cushioned pew, its back and ends ornately carved. They rise simultaneously, as if this has been rehearsed, and simultaneously they bow, a salutation entirely in keeping with the fact that each wears a man's waistcoat above her skirts. (So the rumour that they wear man's dress wholly is untrue.)

"Welcome to Plas Newydd, Mr Wickham," says Lady Eleanor Butler in a voice that contains nothing of a woman's natural desire to intimate that a man's presence is a pleasure to her.

Sarah Ponsonby echoes, "...to Plas Newydd, Mr Wickham," then smiles like one wishing to intimate a private and separate kindness.

Somehow he has no choice but to occupy a low carved chair facing them. It might have been the stool of repentance in some wrong-mongering dissenting meeting-house, but it is not because of conscience that it feels like this, not at all, but only because he supposes that Lydia – perhaps Darcy, too – has represented to these ladies that the man he is now continues to commit his old misdeeds.

"I will not trifle with you. You conceal my wife here."

"We conceal no one," says Lady Eleanor languidly, as though Wickham's accusation has no power to rouse indignation. Her grey hair is short, mannish; she wears some military-style decoration around her neck; her grey eyes hold his like those of a man who challenges you to a duel. He has a sudden absurd picture of he and she exchanging shots in the shrubbery beyond the windows, the other creature simpering around as Lady Eleanor's grotesque second.

"She has been here, that at least I know!" He dilutes his vehemence with wryness. "So foolish a fugitive from her marriage is my wife that she leaves behind the correspondence which prepared the way for her flight."

"Both her hand and her style want improvement," murmurs Sarah conversationally. A stumpy-legged dog, a yappy-looking thing, places insolent paws upon his lap and stares up at him.

"So you admit she *has been* here." Wickham's tone declares *has been* to be a euphemism for *is*.

The kindliness in Sarah's voice is unperturbed. "You must not mind Sappho. She means to welcome you no less sincerely than do we. There is—"

"Sappho!" Wickham is on his feet, dislodging the dog, who gives a series of yapping barks. "So it is as I thought. My wife has been lured to a house of unnatural practices."

"Lured, Mr Wickham?" Eleanor's Irish brogue makes the question flirtatious, if you overlook the magistrate's sternness of her countenance. "My beloved friend was about to say that there is no safe inference from our reading a letter to our sheltering its author."

"I shall not stand for this. The law places my wife under my protection. It shall compel you to give her up. You shall learn the hard way that you cannot trifle with a connection of Darcy of Pemberley, one of the greatest landowners in England."

"Before I learn that," says Eleanor, "I should wish to be enlightened on another matter. We come from Ireland and, living here in sweet retirement, may still be unfamiliar with the manners of this island. Is it the custom here for a gentleman to stand and harangue ladies?"

He cannot say *Yes* and he cannot say *No*, and he feels absurdity spreading out from him like rooks from a roost. He sits down again and Sarah says with ancient sweetness to Eleanor, "I wonder if the gentleman referred to, Mr Darcy, is known to our friend the Duke of Wellington?"

"I think," advises Eleanor in reply, "you might ask the Queen,

41

when you write to her, whether he is known to her."

In the silence Sappho makes little growling lunges at Wickham's boots. He sighs, and when he looks up all the wrath has gone from his face and he is a supplicating boy.

"I most humbly beg your pardon. To rise thus to berate ladies... Pray let me commence my enquiry anew. I confess to you – I declare – that I love my wife. There, you know it. I have, I truly believe, been a good husband to her. It is true that when she was young I was a very Lovelace to her, I polluted her innocence and earned every reproach which Darcy, Mr Darcy, heaped upon me. I have repaid the trust that he placed in me, a trust that some said he placed unwarrantedly. I have repaid it by a reformation of life, of manners, of heart, such that no taint of disgrace can now spread from me to Pemberley. And though I was her seducer, yet..."

He is silent for so long that Sarah gives gentle encouragement: "True honesty creates its own delicacy, whatever may be the facts it discloses."

Reaching for Sappho he lifts her wriggling onto his lap and commences petting that is almost frenzied. "I am not unacquainted with the signs that... that a passion may be entertained for one of one's own sex, for I have looked into the pages of M Diderot and the Comte de Sade, and have, besides, the testimony of my own observations during a voyage with my regiment to Portugal, when I saw enough to understand why a noted wit has remarked that it is no accident that admirals are designated rears and vices. But my wife, my wife, whose beauty no man would scorn..." His face is haggard with pleading, tears stand in his eyes. "Though I confess I was her seducer, yet there was in her no lack of willingness to be seduced. Her witchery, her witching of me, was from the heart." Sappho's teeth making a sudden protest against an over-fierce caress, he cries, "My God, she ran after officers like a damned bitch in heat! I thrashed a man who declared that her petticoat should be the regimental flag. She could not, of her own will, have sought to engage in practices that – that—"

"That men's *damned* gossip attributes to us." Eleanor drolly reproves his use of the word.

"I love my wife, I *know* my wife."

"How very sad," says Sarah, in the voice for commiserating with a village woman over a sick child.

Eleanor muses, "You love her; and so you conclude you know her. Love and knowledge: may they not be distinct existences? Everything is what it is and not another thing, as the celebrated Bishop Butler observed; alas, I have not the honour of his having been a relation of mine. It is a thing on which you might reflect, that a young woman who runs after officers may do so, not because she has an urgent passion for the sex, but because she has no passion for the sex. Such conduct will mask from her friends the fact that the wishes of her heart are not those which the wishes of her friends confer upon her, friends who – as my beloved friend and I know well – may strive to make marriage a fate for her as inescapable as that of those set upon by the press-gang."

"But she was so *proud* to be married." With a bitterness whose cause is unclear, he adds, "Her sister Eliz— Mrs Darcy was quite satirical on the point."

"That, too, may serve the purposes of a mask, both to the world at large and even to her husband."

His face explodes with recognition. "Good God, Mrs Forster, the Colonel's wife, their intimacy that was like an *alliance*." To enforce the oath he brings his hand down fiercely on poor Sappho, who yelps and leaps to the floor. "And Hetty Sawyer! Always there was something that was not... that was not *fitting* between mistress and maidservant, a sly whispering confiding *friendship*, it smacked of, where there could

43

be none. Sometimes, Mrs Wickham wearing servant's dress with her, they would set off like two maidservants making holiday, dining at some low tavern among the lowest. I thought it a mere whim, like that of the late Queen of France to play at being a milkmaid. How deceived I was! And that my wife should seek, should engage in, should do that which… with a common maid of work!"

"Whereas it is a truth universally acknowledged that no gentleman would look with desire on a servant." says Eleanor. "Mr Richardson's *Pamela* is testimony to that."

Like the smell from a farm wench, absurdity again radiates from him until Sarah's manifest benevolence comes to his rescue. "Are you fond of music, Mr Wickham?"

This is so much a hostess's standard conversational ploy that he half expects a harp to be lugged in, perhaps so that the ugly maid without the witch's hat can sing Welsh airs to him.

"Extremely." The guest's standard conversational reply.

"And you are acquainted with Mr Boyce's *Solomon*?" How delicately eager she is for an affirmative reply.

"There you have the advantage of me."

"No safe inference, Mr Wickham." Eleanor, again. "My beloved friend did not say she was acquainted with the work. Merely, she asked you whether *you* knew it. But, yes, we know it. *Solomon* was performed in Dublin and Kilkenny when we were young; Mr Boyce was quite the favourite of music-lovers in our native island. And in *Solomon* there is a remarkable scene. The female, whose lover happens to be male, hears her lover's voice without. She rushes to the door, she opens it with inconceivable rapidity – and no one is there."

"No one." Sarah, encouraging a child learning his letters.

"*No one!*" Eleanor, with damning finality. "Ergo..." Thus she demonstrates that the classical tongues are not the preserve of men only.

He slumps; Sappho snuffles his unwitting dangling fingers. From the luxuriant foliage of the cornice a face sticks out its tongue at him. "Yet I love her still. Swear to me you are not concealing her."

Lady Eleanor is on her feet, ringing a small brass bell that emits a flinchingly loud noise. "You shall not, Mr Wickham, ask a lady to swear to that which she has already told you. Mr Wickham is leaving immediately," she says to the witch-faced servant hastening in.

"I beg your pardon most humbly, but—"

"Immediately." She says it crisply, intimating he is too contemptible to be thundered at; Sarah smiles sweetly at him; the servant curtseys to him.

Cheeks flaming, he is escorted from the room. "Are they always so damned touchy?"

"Always they are most kind to me, sir." She locks eyes on his. The look that he thought was expressive of the stupidity inseparable from ugliness – might it be expressive of something else altogether?

He finds himself murmuring, "Not as kind as I could be."

The way the creature turns away is nothing but a coquettish invitation to place his hand on her waist, but the effect of his touch is merely to hasten her to the door, like soap slipping from a squeezing hand.

She holds the outer door open for him, her eyes again searching his as no servant's should. "Good morning, sir." There is something discomposing in those farewell words, and it is only once he has exited and is beneath the elaborate Gothic porch that he realises what it was: her Welsh accent had vanished entirely. And the pout of her lips had been no longer porcine, and how tall she was, as tall as his beautiful Lydia, and now he has no doubt at all that her bold look, eye to eye – squintless! – had challenged him to the duel that ends in the slaking of passion. Oh yes, this one, too, would run after officers, and he turns to make a fresh inspection of her. But the door is already shut, or almost so, and when he pushes on it to reopen it, it swings open without resistance and no one is there.

Hurrying to his inn without a backward glance at this poisoned house – no, he does not hurry, his pace is merely a soldier's fast march – he seems to hear laughter, which must be the cawing of rooks in the trees beyond Plas Newydd.

In the library there is indeed laughter, a great bark of it from Eleanor. "And he knew you not?"

"It was a risk we ought not to have taken." The Hon Sarah, in a voice of delicate and completely forgiving reproach. She gives a giggle of surprising coarseness.

They watch as the wimple-like covering is pulled from tumbling blonde hair and the servant manner, too, is thrown off. "Oh, it is a good trick. How my sister Kitty will laugh when I tell her! I was in no danger, no danger at all. Yet he had every chance to discover me if he would. I looked directly in his face many times and was sure he must know me, and then I stood at the door in his full view the entire time until he passed beyond the gate, and though he looked back, la! he knew not his wife."

Laughing noisily, all restraint abandoned, Lydia throws herself between the ladies on the pew-like bench, an arm around each neck. Sappho, front paws up, nuzzles her lap.

❧

My inspiration: I found intriguing the fact that Jane Austen and the Ladies of Llangollen were contemporaries. Did they know of each other?

EMPTY HANDS

Rebecca Rouillard

Empty Hands

❧

Rebecca Rouillard

It is a truth universally acknowledged that old age brings fitful sleep. Elizabeth Bennet rarely sleeps soundly. She dreams, if you can call it a dream, that she has something precious in her hands that she is trying to hold on to, though it keeps slipping away. Just before dawn she becomes convinced that she has a firm grip on it, but then she wakes with empty hands and a lingering sense of loss, her fingers clenched in useless fists.

She sits on the side of her bed and flexes her fingers gingerly. Her left hand is slightly less contorted so she uses that one to bend back each of the fingers of her right hand – very gently, one at a time. It is agony at first but as she moves her hands the pain eases a little. She stretches and rubs her hands together for a while until she can comfortably grip the edge of the bed and push herself into a standing position. She lets her breath catch up with her for a moment as she contemplates her next move.

The nurse bustles in. "Morning dearie, need a hand to the loo?"

"No thank you. I'm on my way."

"You sure?"

"I'm fine. Thank you."

49

She treads carefully, as though her feet might shatter if they encounter the floor too abruptly. She negotiates the dressing table with its bruising edges and escapes into the bathroom. It's decorated in the same insistently cheerful floral style as the bedroom. She doesn't remember what her favourite colour is but she is quite sure that it is not yellow. The mindless optimism of yellow makes her want to bang her head against the wall. But she knows that they mean well – her carers, her captors. This prison is not of their making – their culpability is limited to the decor.

Her dentures lurk in their container next to the sink. She rinses them and puts them in her mouth. She regards her teeth in the mirror – pearly white, perfectly aligned, conformed. She is like these teeth. Everything that made her unique has been worn away, filed to fit some convenient mould, and she has forgotten the shape of the discarded pieces. The face in the mirror is no help – it's familiar but still strange. Where did this wispy, white hair come from, this furrowed and folded skin? She does not recognise herself.

"I think I used to have a gap between my front teeth," she tells the nurse who is stripping the sheets from her bed.

"Did you really?"

"Yes. I always hated it and I wanted to get rid of it but Sam liked it. He thought it was sexy."

The nurse stops, a bundle of sheets in her arms. "Did you say Sam? You remembered Sam?"

"No. I don't know why I said that. I don't know who that is."

"Are you sure? Just think about it for a moment, you said that Sam thought the gap in your teeth was sexy."

"I don't know. I don't remember." She is flustered, betrayed by her tongue. She doesn't know who Sam is. It makes her anxious that her mouth remembers something that her brain doesn't.

"It's all right dearie. Don't worry about it. I just thought you might have remembered something."

"No, I don't remember."

If she is honest with herself she barely remembers anything. She has no recall of any place other than this – the floral confines of her day-to-day life. She knows that her name is Elizabeth Bennet, though the doctor calls her something else. She doesn't know why they try to confuse her by calling her by another name. There seems to be some conspiracy involved. She is quite sure that she has a sister called Jane but she hasn't seen her for a long time. There is a picture of the two of them as children on her dressing table – one blonde, one brunette, both wearing pink dresses, holding hands, smiling. Those smiles make her feel happy and sad at the same time. These children are more aware, more secure in their own space than she is, despite the decades that separate them. There is a whole life out there somewhere that she has been parted from. It is like she has lost a conjoined twin. If she can somehow recall the circumstances of this operation then they will be reunited. There is one other thing she knows for certain – she knows that she is betrothed to a man called Mr Darcy, although she doesn't know what has happened to him. The nurses will not tell her anything about him and the doctor answers her questions with questions of his own. She hides this knowledge in her heart and she waits for him. One day he will come and save her from this place.

When she is dressed the nurse fetches her for breakfast. Eating is mechanical these days. She has no preferences and no appetite. She eats a little of what is put in front of her for the duration of the allocated time. After breakfast the nurse takes her through to the sitting room. The man is already waiting there for her. He comes to visit her nearly every day. Once he'd tried to kiss her cheek when he arrived but it had made her uncomfortable so he hadn't tried it again.

"Morning. How did you sleep?"

"Well, thank you. And how are you?"

"I'm very well."

He is tall but slightly stooped, his hair is white and he has a nice smile. He also has unusual eyes – one is brown and one is green. They are a little disconcerting but she feels that she can trust him.

"Are we going to read today?"

"Yes please."

"I have Katherine Mansfield."

"You always bring short stories."

"Don't you like short stories?"

"I do like them, I think. I was just wondering."

"I'll bring you something else if you prefer, but with short stories at least we always get to the end. I don't like to leave you hanging."

He gets his reading glasses out and begins to read to her. He doesn't always read. Sometimes he talks to her about his children. He shows her pictures of them. They'd even been to visit her once – two young women. They'd brought pictures too – of their children. She doesn't know why people keep showing her pictures of children. She'd been polite to them but she prefers it when it is just the two of them. She likes it when he reads to her. His voice soothes her. When he is with her it doesn't seem to matter that she can't remember. She is lulled into a false sense of familiarity. But today she waits until there is no one else in the room then she stops him by laying her hand on his arm. He looks up from the book.

"I'm sorry, I just wanted to ask you something."

"You can ask me anything."

"Thank you. What I wanted to ask you is... do you know where Mr Darcy is?"

The man looks sad for a moment. What does he know? Has something happened?

She continues quickly. "We are engaged, but I don't know where he's gone. I don't want to ask the nurses again, I don't think they believe me." She is sure that he knows something. He looks down at his hands and then back at her.

"Can I tell you a secret?" He leans towards her.

"Yes." She holds her breath.

He winks. "I am Mr Darcy."

She turns her head away from him, engulfed in disappointment. The spark of hope that had been ignited is extinguished. He is just part of the system, another conspirator – cushioning her, patronising her, placating her. She is tired. She doesn't have the energy to take it further.

"I'm sorry. I know that's not what you wanted to hear. I don't know what else to tell you."

"Keep reading, please."

He opens the book again and carries on with the story. She listens for a while but then she closes her eyes. They are tired and the morning sun is making them water. The floral wallpaper pattern dances persistently behind her eyelids. His voice fades.

"Miss Elizabeth Bennet, I beg your pardon, would you mind terribly if I ravished you?"

She is lying in bed reading *Pride and Prejudice*, her pillow propped up behind her head. The morning sun, filtered by leaves, is stippled on the white duvet cover. She is warm, comfortable. The satin of her pyjamas slides luxuriously against her skin. She puts her book down and turns to her husband. He has just woken up. His hair is sticking up unevenly, endearingly. He leans across the bed and reaches for her.

"Mr Darcy, you're not behaving in a very gentlemanlike manner!" She flutters her eyelashes at him coyly.

"I'm sorry Miss Bennet, I just can't help myself."

She giggles. "Shhh, you'll wake the girls."

He growls in the back of his throat and then rubs his stubble against her face.

"Ow! You beast, stop it!" she laughs helplessly and tries to push him away.

"Who's going to wake the girls now?"

She shrieks and beats him off with her pillow.

"Why are you hitting Daddy, Mummy?" A sleepy voice interrupts. There are two little figures in pink pyjamas – one blonde, one brunette, standing by the bed.

"Can we play too?"

"Of course you can. Hop on."

The little girls jump on the bed gleefully and launch themselves into the assault. She looks at her husband, her beautiful girls. He smiles back at her – he has such an amazing smile, she thinks. And his eyes, so startling – one brown, one green.

He winks at her. "Love you."

"Love you too, Sam."

She opens her eyes. He is there, watching her. At first she can't speak. The reality of this rediscovered life is a solid object – obstructing her airway. She gasps for air.

"Are you all right?" He leans forward and grips her hand in concern. When she looks down he remembers himself and starts to take his hand away. She grabs his hand with her own.

"Sam."

Now he is the one who cannot speak, he can only smile and smile at her.

"Sam, I remembered. The girls? Where are the girls?"

"They're fine, they're fine. I'll call them, maybe then can get here in time, before... I brought them to see you, do you remember?"

"I remember. I have a picture of them in my room don't I? How long have I been here Sam? What's happening to me?"

"It's been two years. You have Alzheimer's, my love."

"But I remember now, I remember everything."

"Yes, that's wonderful. I'm so happy."

"You said you would call the girls and maybe they would be able to get here in time… so it won't last?"

"I'm afraid not."

"I'm going to forget you again?"

"Yes."

"Oh Sam, how do you cope with this? I didn't know who you were?"

"You were waiting for me though. You thought it was Mr Darcy you were waiting for but you were waiting."

"I was waiting."

"You always did love that book."

"I love you Sam, I love you so much. I'm so sorry I forgot you."

"It's not your fault, my love."

It's not her fault. It's out of her control. She finally understands the extent of the thing she has been trying to hold on to, this life. Everything that was vague and fuzzy has been brought into focus. It is something worth clinging to. But her memory sustains it like a fistful of sand – in this moment of clarity it is gritty and substantial but it is so hard to hold on to. It will slip away again soon enough and she will be adrift once again, with empty hands.

She grips her husband's hands tighter. "Don't let me go Sam."

"I won't let you go." He promises.

※

My inspiration: Mr Darcy has become a literary romantic ideal although this was not necessarily Jane Austen's intention – she often undermined and satirised fictional heroes. In response to this, *Empty Hands* explores the heroism of ordinary people.

PERSUADED

Rebecca Lees

Persuaded

୫୯

Rebecca Lees

It was all Gok Wan's fault. Well, his and Beth Elliot's. My best friend
Beth, 29 and in possession of the "I'll do anything, me," kind of
exuberance that lands everyone within striking distance right in the
sticky stuff. Or, in our case, right in the sticky stuff and with barely
a stitch on.

"Oh come *on* girls, it's for *charity*," Beth persuaded, as if we were
a right bunch of modern-day Ebenezers. I wouldn't have minded but
I *work* for a charity, for goodness sake – one of the largest cancer ones
in the country, as it happens. And then there's Maria. Now, no one
can say that Maria Mossgrave's intentions aren't in the right place.
It's just that her conviction doesn't always match up to them. Last
year she did a sky dive for the British Heart Foundation; a worthy
choice, except that the BHF probably spent more on the paramedics
who administered to Maria afterwards than the two and a half
grand she raised in the first place. Anyway, the point is that our little
gang is as averagely generous as the next – however, we prefer to do
our Just Giving with our clothes on.

As reasonably stated by Laura. Gorgeous Laura Russell, who,
ironically, had the very least in Beth's plan to worry about.

"I mean, naked?" she repeated. "Couldn't we keep *something* on?"

"Well, no, seeing as it's a *naked* calendar. Duh!" Beth rolled immaculately lashed eyes. "Don't worry, though, we're expected to bring props to cover our wobbly bits. Which brings me onto the theme..." She paused for emphasis, or perhaps in hope that the Cadbury's gorilla would make an appearance and perform a drum roll. We stared at her, suitably open-mouthed.

"Climbing gear!" Beth announced. "A harness here, some belays there – it will be brilliant!"

I glanced at Maria's generous frame and tried to dismiss the notion that perhaps a whole climbing wall would be more apt. We had started indoor climbing a couple of months ago, another of Beth's brainwaves. She had decided we needed more "quality time" together, just "the girls". Quick translation: newly single Beth needed some stooges to help her check out hot men at the climbing centre, which explained how we found ourselves dangling twenty feet up Grade Four routes every Monday night while Beth strutted about the bouldering corner eyeing up her latest targets.

"But aren't naked calendars a bit, well, past their sell-by?" I enquired. "Haven't we moved on since then?" I could see Beth hadn't factored all these questions into The Plan.

"Anna, we're hardly the Mothers' Union are we!" she snapped, and I opted against asking if she meant the WI. "Look, Gok's a cultural phenomenon! He's transformed the way we feel about ourselves! That's what the *Cardiff Leader* is basing the competition on. They want 12 inspirational, empowered and, of course, attractive groups, one for each month. There's a holiday in the Seychelles for the group voted for by readers as cover material! Oh, and all proceeds will go to the winning group's chosen charity." Beth tried to look worthy but the gleam in her eyes suggested she had already selected beachwear from the Next Directory.

*

The first part was all very simple; we just had to take some snaps of us in action at the climbing wall (clothes on) and email them to *Leader* with our group name and a 50-word tiebreaker. "The Boulder Holders," Laura had suggested, grinning, when we brainstormed the name. Maria and I fell about and even Beth flashed a smile, although I could tell she was gutted she hadn't thought of it first.

No one other than Beth expected to hear any more about it but, to our surprise – and horror – the eye-catching name, Beth's highly polished tiebreaker and photos of Laura in miniscule climbing shorts proved an irresistible combo to the *Leader's* editorial team. We were to be September Beth announced to us, and her 337 other Facebook friends, with glee. Before we had time to say "figure of eight", we were assembled in the *Leader's* boardroom clad – for now – in rather flimsy white cheesecloth robes.

"I can't believe we're doing this," said Laura, staring around the room at similarly cheese-clothed strangers helping themselves to teas and coffees. "Honestly Beth, this is *it* – no more bright ideas, OK?"

"Hmmm." Beth nodded but clearly wasn't listening, staring instead around the room at the competition. "Right, I've done my homework and, as far as I can see, the ones we need to worry about are Dubs Be Good to Me. They're into VWs; got old Beetles and campervans and what-nots." She gestured towards a quartet of women laughing over the tops of polystyrene cups. "That must be them. And those women by the water cooler, they're a local craft group called Without a Stitch, I think." She sniffed. "They look a bit knit-your-own-yoghurts to me. Don't think we've got much to—"

"Bethan, *sweetie!*" Beth was halted by a middle-aged man springing towards her, arms pedalling. Maria, Laura and I had never seen him before but we guessed he was William Walters, director of a local am-dram group called UpStaged! (their exclamation mark, not mine). Beth's firm had done some PR for their outdoor performances last summer and she had entertained us with several impressions of Mr Walters; the other thing Beth Elliot was in possession of, other than a facility for bright ideas, was a rather hard-boiled but very accurate wit.

Vanity was the beginning and end of Mr Walters' character. He had been remarkably convinced of being handsome in his youth and at 54 was assured (by himself) he was still a very fine man. Few women could think more of their personal appearance than he did; indeed, the chances of the actresses in UpStaged! getting as much mirror-time in the arts centre dressing room appeared very slim indeed. He had chosen a Cleopatra theme for his group's photo shoot, necessitating the marble-effect columns and huge earthenware jugs now being heaved about by the actors. Also required were some grapes, which Mr Walters was managing to carry himself. I hardly dared think about the asp.

While Mr Walters acted out his creative vision to Beth, I took another look around the room. Suddenly I nudged Laura. "Hey, look at the guys over there!" I said. Laura followed my gaze and grinned.

"How on earth did Beth miss them off her shortlist?" she said. "Her radar must be slipping! Ooh, check out the blond one. And look at the biceps on the guy sitting down!" Five or six men in their twenties and early thirties were sitting on plush sofas next to the tea machine. All muscle and tans, they must, I judged, be from a gym or football club.

"I'll be voting for them!" I said. "C'mon, time for that cuppa!"

Just as we started in the direction of the group, however, the door opened and in were shepherded a gaggle of robe-wearing men carrying crash helmets. "Thank you, Hal's Angels," said the editorial assistant overseeing proceedings. She spoke cheerily but a slightly stunned look in her eyes suggested she had seen more than she was ready for. "Right then, if we could have Services with a Smile next, please!"

I saw Beth brighten as she clocked the men Laura and I had been eyeing up. Then almost instantly she flushed and turned abruptly back to Mr Walters. Puzzled, I looked from her to the group now making their way towards the door. It all clicked into place. *Services,* of course. These guys were in the forces – and had obviously seen some action. Closer up, I could see the one with blond hair had a harsh scar running from his ear across his cheek. Another, wearing jogging bottoms rather than a robe, was walking stiffly and I realised he had a prosthetic leg. The man Laura had pointed to had not been in a seat but a wheelchair, the rippling arms now propelling him along with ease.

As the men squeezed past us he flashed a quick smile in our direction, lighting up Bambi-brown eyes that seemed to belie the strapping frame folded into the wheelchair. They were the kind of eyes that Beth would usually melt into, but she was busy trying to re-engage Mr Walters in conversation. He, however, was not listening. While most people were watching the servicemen with friendly encouragement, Mr Walters was scrutinising them with an unashamed stare. Before they were quite out of the door he turned to Beth and said in a too-loud whisper: "You know, soldiers grow old sooner than any other men. They're exposed to all kinds of weather in Afghanistan till their skin is hardly fit to be seen!"

There was a horrified silence, broken only by the man with Bambi eyes, who glanced at Mr Walters over his shoulder.

"Well, we'd better pack our factor 50 for that trip to the Seychelles then," he said cheerfully and, with a neat manoeuvre, was out of the door.

Beth, guilty by association with the culprit, at least had the decency to look mortified. Mr Walters, however, was unrepentant.

"What?" he demanded of the bikers, who were looking at him in disgust. "I only meant their skin, nothing else." But the buzz of nervous excitement in the boardroom had evaporated and the remainder of our wait was gloomy, each group closing ranks and no longer bantering with their neighbours.

An eternity later, it was our turn. We filed into the gleaming white studio, spotlights glaring at us. The photographer, we were relieved to discover, was a woman, friendly but with the professional briskness of one with a deadline-filled morning. "Right ladies, what have we got here?" she asked, and we held up our props for examination. "OK then, let's get to work!" she exclaimed. There was a pause as we waited for Lesley, as identified by her staff pass, to manoeuvre us into position. She returned our expectant looks. "Er, the robes, ladies?" she suggested.

Beth was first to oblige and we all sheepishly followed, wishing the lights were more forgiving and our tiny beige thongs more substantial. We couldn't quite look at each other as Lesley busied herself stringing ropes around Maria and getting Laura to lie on her stomach on the floor, face up and hugging her climbing shoes to her chest. I was perched on a stool, modesty protected by a tangle of harnesses which I had to pretend to untie, while Beth, to her chagrin, was relegated to a step ladder in the background, a couple of rungs up and peering over the top.

"God, glad that's done," Laura sighed as, robes back on, we were deposited at the boardroom door.

"I know, I can breathe out again now!" said Maria. I had expected to feel the rush of relief and elation I got after climbing a particularly tricky new route but instead we were all completely flat. Mr Walters' words hung over us and, no longer even tempted by the remaining pastries laid out on the boardroom table, we made our way to the tiny office allocated as our dressing room, got into our clothes and quietly returned to the mundane rhythm of our lives.

By the calendar's launch four weeks later, however, we had perked up. We even had the excitement of planning what to wear this time. We arrived at the Parc Hotel fizzing and were shown into a grand function room draped in silver and hot pink. Maria squealed and pointed to giant prints adorning the walls. There we were, enormous and vivid in our Photoshopped glory, staring alluringly back at ourselves. We looked surprisingly glamorous and I had to admit this might have been one of Beth's better ideas after all.

We had been placed on a table with the bikers and Dubs Be Good to Me, a good-natured bunch who became increasingly raucous as the free wine flowed. By the time dessert arrived, one was gaily recounting the tale of an errant tyre that had rolled away from her at exactly the wrong moment during the shoot. "Obviously that's the cover sorted!" a voice behind me said and I turned and found myself staring straight into those brown eyes, their owner parked remarkably close to my own chair.

"Oh, you can't have seen our pictures yet!" I fired back. "A couple of spare tyres have got nothing on our belay devices!" The VW girls laughed good-humouredly.

"Oh, I've been studying your photo very carefully," came the reply. "All in the name of art, obviously. Not bad, but I think you need a bit of help with your technique. I used to rock climb, as it happens."

The editor of the *Leader* chose that moment to tap the microphone into life and read out, to a babble of excitement, a message of support for the calendar from Gok Wan's office. Then she made an attempt at looking sombre; quite some feat given the amount of wine I had seen her knocking back just minutes earlier.

"Unfortunately, I have some unpleasant news before I announce the cover group," she said. "We have had to take the decision to disqualify one group due to, um, opinions contrary to those of the editorial team." I looked around the room and realised I hadn't seen Mr Walters and his UpStaged! posse.

"So we have decided that the cover group will have *two* months in the calendar," continued the editor. "And that group is..." (There was a pause worthy of Philip Schofield at the exciting bit of *Dancing on Ice*.) "Services with a Smile!" A huge cheer went up and the lads did their best to look surprised and modest, although they could hardly have failed to be aware of the massive Facebook campaign set up by fans to boost their votes.

As the dancing got underway, I inched my way to Services With a Smile's table and pulled up a chair next to Bambi eyes.

"Well, the best men won," I smiled. "Listen, about the day of the photo shoot..."

"Yes, yes, it was all your fault and you need to apologise." The answer took me aback but those eyes were still smiling. "Well, nothing short of dinner for two will make up for it, really."

"OK," I laughed. "If that's what it takes, I suppose I have no choice."

"There's a condition, mind," he said. "I'm trusting you to keep your clothes on this time." The chocolate eyes sparkled a challenge.

I picked up the delicately crafted place name in front of his plate and ran a finger along the top.

"Well, Captain Wentworth," I said. "I'm not sure I can be persuaded to promise that."

꩜

My inspiration: *Persuasion* is my favourite Austen novel and several of its themes still resonate, such as our obsession with appearance and the quiet heroism of the Forces. I wanted to update these themes whilst attempting to capture some of the sparkle and humour of *Persuasion*. The opinions of pantomime villain Mr Walters show the gulf between our everyday worries and the real challenges faced by our servicemen and women.

FAIRY-TALE ENDING

Colette O'Connor

Fairy-tale Ending

&

Colette O'Connor

It was a Sunday. The boiler had broken during the night and Charlotta Lukov watched the sunrise curled into as tight a ball as possible under a clammy blanket. The grey haze of day caught in the fog of her breath and sketched her outline on the wall. The flat was always damp; the ceilings were watermarked and windowsills grew mould unless regularly scrubbed. Frost would creep across the inner face of the windowpanes like lace. Up there on the fourteenth floor on stormy days the wind boomed curiously and rattled the windows until they seemed likely to shatter. Sometimes it felt like being on a ship in the middle of the ocean; it was easy to imagine the washing on the balconies filling out like sails, propelling the whole estate off the edge of the world.

She mostly kept indoors, despite the discomfort, to avoid the journey to and from the flat; drunks often congregated on the stairs, and sometimes local teenagers would shout abuse or spit at her. Her younger self would have returned the curses, but the English words matching her feelings were elusive in the heat of the moment. Because of this, it was more shame than fear that made her dread running into them again. As getting paid work was not a legal option for her, she broke the shapelessness of the days with a strict housework regime. The radio was her most treasured possession, and sometimes she stopped what she was doing to dance, eyes closed. Music had a way of bringing back the good memories of her old life which would otherwise stay buried. She remembered her old apartment full of photographs, and nights spent in the heaving darkness of clubs singing along with the music, her voice being drowned out. Salt on her skin, hands around her waist.

But that day the cold had worked its way into her muscles and she was too stiff to dance. She tried phoning a friend, hoping for an invitation to lunch, but got no answer. With no money and nowhere else to go, she decided to go to the Sunday service at the nearest church in order to get warm.

The church was a modern one, boxy and concrete, squatting in the shadows of the tower blocks at the edge of the estate. Charlotta was not religious, but visited each Thursday when the church was used as a drop-in centre for asylum seekers. She had come to Glasgow alone, but had quickly become close to the Scottish woman who ran the group. Elizabeth Bennet was only in her mid-twenties, younger than Charlotta, but her intelligence and stubbornness were formidable and she was considered a valuable ally in any battle against the Home Office. Charlotta was now, for the second time, appealing for her right to stay in Britain.

As a child she had regularly attended the village Russian Orthodox church, and found St Mary's extremely plain in comparison. The bare walls reminded her of the stories her grandmother had told her, of gold and icons being stripped from Orthodox churches in the thirties. Nor was the vicar an imposing man. He was short and stocky, and had a bald patch which was inexpertly concealed with a gelled comb-over. If he felt any passion for his sermon, it was masked by a naturally flat and nasal voice, which seemed to have left some of the elderly parishioners in a trance. The drone was audible throughout, even when the congregation was called on to sing "Jerusalem".

When the service finished, she was reluctant to join the people streaming towards the door, with the cold flat waiting for her. The vicar saw her hovering in the aisle, and caught her eye.

"I couldnae help but notice you're new to St Mary's. I'm Reverend Collins. William," he said, offering her a slightly sweaty hand.

"Charlotta Lukov."

"Welcome. I'm amazed so many made it along today – very cold outside."

"Oh. Yes. And inside," she joked. "My boiler is broken."

Reverend Collins expressed horror at the thought and invited her to join him for a cup of tea. It was strange meeting him in the flesh. He had been the subject of Elizabeth's jokes ever since his attempt to flirt with her at a charity fundraiser. It was a story she delighted in retelling, always concluding with, "I must have been mad to turn him down. There's nothing sexier than a 43-year-old Casanova who still lives with his mother!"

Away from the pulpit Collins seemed to struggle for words, as if he was used to reading the Bible as an autocue for life and without it lacked the necessary skills for conversation. He observed her unblinkingly over the rim of his mug, giving her the sensation of being covered by small moving insects. She pulled up her neckline to hide her cleavage; he blushed and looked away.

"Where do ye come from, originally," he asked finally.

"Russia."

"I thought so. Your eyes remind me of the Volga river." A self-satisfied smile. Whether this was supposed to be a romantic sentiment was unclear; he just seemed proud to have produced such poetry.

"Grey and cold?" Charlotta replied, willing herself not to laugh.

"Free."

She wondered whether Collins had used the silent minutes of tea drinking to invent this fantastical compliment, or whether he had got it from a book, and had been looking for many years for a Russian woman to try it out on.

"Have you been to Russia, Reverend?"

"No, but my ma went once and took lots of photos. She's a brilliant photographer. Could have gone professional, if she hadn't other talents to concentrate on."

Once he had started on the subject of his mother, nothing could divert him. Elizabeth had named him "Reverend Oedipus" with good reason. Charlotta's exotic eyes were quickly forgotten, to her relief.

The widowed Mrs Catherine Collins was apparently an eminent member of the community who sat on the boards of several local charities. It took a good ten minutes for the Reverend to get over the shock of finding that Charlotta had not heard of her. When he spoke of his mother, his voice took on a warmth that had been absent before. The conversation turned into an extended monologue with no input needed from Charlotta, and she found her mind wandering. Keeping up the appearance of interest was extremely tiresome.

She had never met a person like Collins before. He obviously lacked awareness of how people perceived him – either that or he had a truly impervious ego. Surely he must have noticed over the years that everyone he met spurned his company? Everyone except his mother, she supposed.

Rather than the scorn he inspired in Elizabeth, her enduring emotion from the encounter was one of pity. The problem was that feeling sympathy for Collins did not render his company more pleasant.

*

Charlotta's engagement party was a quiet affair: a dinner arranged in the best possible tastes by Catherine Collins. Elizabeth was there for moral support, as Charlotta had the feeling that she was not liked by her prospective mother-in-law. The Reverend called this idea nonsense but Charlotta still had the sneaking suspicion that the whole meal had been set up as some kind of test. The main course was lobster, something she was unaccustomed to, and came with its own special cutlery. While she struggled to extract the flesh, Catherine raised one sharply drawn eyebrow in her son's direction, as if to indicate proof of a previously made point.

"Pass me the salt please, Charlotte dear," she said. Elizabeth shot a look at Charlotta. Charlotta smiled tightly and handed over the salt without a word.

"Mrs Collins, her name is Charlotta," said Elizabeth on cue. Charlotta felt a hot embarrassment clutch her stomach and fixed her eyes on the table.

"I was just using the British version of the name. I've never heard *her* complain. After all, isn't she supposed to be British now she's marrying my son?" Catherine struggled to maintain her saccharine tone, unused to being challenged.

Collins, oblivious to the mounting antagonism between his mother and Elizabeth and the humiliation radiating from the bowed head of his fiancée, announced a toast.

"To my future wife! Who would have thought I'd ever be making this speech! You know," he turned towards the others confidentially, "I wasn't even sure that she loved me until the day I proposed."

"Darling, you are far too self-deprecating. She's very lucky to have you," said his mother.

"So what convinced you?" asked Elizabeth. Her voice was brittle, not her own.

"She told me I had saved her. And what man could possibly resist that?"

The proposal happened soon after Charlotta got a letter from the Home Office, informing her that her appeal had failed. She had no fresh evidence left to present.

When she got home from church that Sunday, she phoned Elizabeth.

"I lost my appeal."

A pause, then: "We'll keep on fighting."

"Collins asked me to marry him."

"What? Reverend Collins? Fuck! I mean, that's unbelievable! God… to take advantage of your position, to——"

"I said yes." She put the phone down.

Thinking back on that phone call, Charlotta hated her own cowardice. How easy it was to play the victim, to paint Collins as the seducer. Easy, but dishonest.

The fear of deportation had her in a quicksand hold. More and more, she found everyday tasks near impossible. When combing her hair, she would forget what she was doing until she felt blood on her forehead and realised it was hers. The songs on the radio just sounded like noise. Then sleep became impossible and getting up felt pointless. She lay in impotent silence, sense of time lost, trapped in an endless cycle of fevered thought.

It had taken her a while after meeting Collins before she was able to admit to herself that she had begun to think of him as a back-up plan. Why else would she keep on going back to church long after the boiler got fixed, and repeating that first awkward tea party, week after week? When merely getting dressed was exhausting… At first she liked to imagine she was paying a kindness to a fellow outsider, or that she was trying to get out of the house more often.

He proved so easy to manipulate. His hunger for flattery knew no bounds. Lying next to him in her dark bedroom for the first time, the disgust in her head was so loud she was afraid that he could hear it. Instead he commented affectionately on her shyness.

Deception did not come naturally, but it got easier, and with him she learnt how to achieve a distance from her own body, to look on coldly as a pathologist. The novelty of horror wore off; guilt took its place. She began to recognise Collins as a peculiarly vulnerable person she was exploiting. There was only one way to live with it: making a bargain with her conscience. She would not abandon Collins as soon as her British passport came through. She would do her best to be his wife.

Elizabeth drove Charlotta back to the estate after her engagement party. It was late, and the air was heavy as if preparing for rain.

"I know you don't love him," said Elizabeth as they paused at the traffic lights.

"Is it obvious?"

"Not to him."

"Good. He's convinced himself he loves me. I need him to believe it."

"Jesus, will you listen to yourself?"

"I cannot afford to be romantic, Lizzie."

Elizabeth shifted impatiently in her seat. "I just don't understand how you can do it. I mean – stuck in a house with that man! Seeing that man sit back every day while his mother sneers at you… How will you stand it? Do you really think you can be that person?"

"Visa whore," said Charlotta, sardonically. A lorry passed and in the flash of the headlights she examined her bitten fingernails.

"I didn't say that. I wouldn't say that."

"That is what Mrs Collins says, I think, when I am not there. Do you hate me?"

"Of course I don't. I'm sorry," she said wearily, "I guess I'm just disappointed."

"Why?"

"I've always admired you, the way you've fought. Not many people would be brave enough. Certainly not me. I would have given up long before."

"So you have not forgotten why I left home, why I cannot go back? The Home Office will not give me a visa. I must get one somehow."

"By marrying Collins! You might as well be in prison. What's the point of it? Talk to your lawyer about a fresh claim. Please don't give up now."

"I am so tired of living in purgatory. I just want to live a life. With Collins, I know what the future is: I will have a home, here. A job. Even children, perhaps. That is enough, no?"

"What about love?"

Charlotta made no answer. Elizabeth fell into silence. There was nothing left to be said, now they knew how it was going to end.

❧

My inspiration: Asylum seekers live economically and socially precarious lives analogous to those of Elizabeth and Charlotte in *Pride and Prejudice*, whose futures are uncertain without marriage. I propose that the compromise Charlotte makes in marrying the undesirable Mr Collins to free her future is far more heroic than Elizabeth's romance as it requires a battle between selfhood and safety. Her pragmatic approach requires a strength that in the end is never needed by the romantic heroine Elizabeth.

IN THE WAY OF HAPPINESS

Marybeth Ihle

In the Way of Happiness

❧

Marybeth Ihle

George Howard stepped out of the door of his lodgings at No. 3 Gower Street, bleary-eyed yet thankful to be alive. The wind was picking up, and it was bitterly cold for October. Pulling his overcoat tightly around him, he headed down the steps, surveying the damage from the night before.

The air raid siren had sounded a little before eleven, and George had made his way down several flights of stairs and out of the back door, where he climbed into the cramped Anderson shelter he had helped construct. His landlady, Mrs Haggerty, was already there, handing out cups of tea, which she poured from a Thermos. George had returned to his bed by two o'clock, once the muffled sounds of explosions had finally died away.

This morning, as he made his way to work, he was surprised to find a gaping hole where his favorite bookshop had once stood on Charing Cross Road. The rubble of bricks and glass was littered with burnt pages. A few passers-by stopped and offered words of encouragement to Mr Pritchard, the proprietor, while George stood in the middle of the pavement, oblivious to everyone who knocked into him. His attention was arrested by the sight of one volume in particular, remarkably intact. Lifting it out of the debris, as dust and small bits of brick fell away, he was not surprised to see the title *Persuasion* written across its spine. It put him in mind of the edition he had first read years ago, during the last war.

Poor health, which had plagued him since boyhood, kept him away from the front lines then, but he had done his part as a hospital porter in Wandsworth. He had been surprised when, during one of his shifts, a doctor had asked him to read to a soldier, badly wounded and suffering from shock. "He's had a rough time of it. Injured at the Somme. This seems to comfort him," the doctor added, pressing *Persuasion* into George's hand. It was an introduction that had lasted a lifetime. As the years went on, he developed a special affection for Miss Anne Elliot, a young lady who had lost her bloom. He wasn't sure if men had blooms they could lose, but if they did, his had certainly abandoned him years ago.

"Go ahead and take it, Mr Howard," said Mr Pritchard, interrupting George's reflections. He reached into his pocket for a few coins. "No, no," said Mr Pritchard absentmindedly before returning to the damage and the finality of his life's work.

George tucked the volume into the breast pocket of his coat and continued on his way down Charing Cross Road. A thought came to him as he waited to cross the street. Doing the sums quickly, he realised he was older than all of the heroes in Miss Austen's novels. He had been close to Edmund Bertram and Edward Ferrars in age when he first read those novels, and he was certainly younger than Mr Darcy and Captain Wentworth when he had read the others. Now it struck him that not only was he older than Mr Knightley and Colonel Brandon, but he had a few years on both of them. He wasn't quite complaining of rheumatism and hadn't taken to wearing flannel waistcoats, but if Marianne Dashwood thought Colonel Brandon old merely at the age of thirty-five, what would she think of him, George Howard, a man in his fifth decade of life? Of course, Marianne had changed her opinion of the poor colonel – illness tends to sober the young, he thought – but there was no reckless and passionate young woman in George's life to return him to his youth. Was there a male equivalent of spinster? Another more frightening thought overtook him: not very far in the future, he'd be as old as Mr Woodhouse. Must he acquire a taste for gruel in the intervening years?

By this time George had reached his desk in the War Office and mechanically went about reviewing ration tallies. It was boring work if he was perfectly honest, with no challenge or change from day to day, but he did it for King and Country. Today, however, after a few minutes of trying to focus on the number of meat rations the butchers on the Fulham Road were taking in, he let his mind wander to the book in his coat pocket. Shutting his door, he slid the book out and opened it to a random page. His eyes fell to a familiar passage:

A man does not recover from such a devotion of the heart to such a woman. He ought not; he does not.

The small diamond ring thrust into George's hands by his mother as she lay dying in the winter of '21 still remained in its velvet box, buried beneath a stack of handkerchiefs in the top drawer of his bureau. He had never come close to using it. George had long ago discovered that he did not possess the talent for inspiring affection. And without wanting it to, his mind fell to one particular evening in his past, an evening he strove to forget but never could.

It had been the night of a dance in Tunbridge Wells, held each year to raise money for the widows left behind from the Great War. George had been young then, only twenty-five, and when he wasn't busy selling boosters he spent his time watching the couples dance. When Martin Chester came to take over his shift, George had refrained from dancing, preferring instead to hang back where the wallflowers sat. Every once in a while, he would catch the eye of one of them and then quickly look away. It was silly, he knew, not to be able to go up to a woman he didn't know and ask her to dance, but the River Avon might as well have been between him and the smiling redhead who was discreetly tapping her foot in time with the music. It just seemed too difficult. What was he to say to a woman? Make a comment about the size of the room? Remark on the number of couples? Was that all it took?

Later that night, as the dance was coming to a close, George was waiting for Martin near the cloakroom. He suddenly found himself standing right next to the smiling redheaded woman and, as before, he could not think of a single word to say to her. As the gentleman next to her handed her her things, a scarf fell to the floor, and George instantly picked it up. "Thank you," she said in a sweet, lovely voice, the tone of which George somehow still remembered after all these years. In the next moment, without any outward sign, without any word uttered, George knew, he *knew* the lady wanted him to assist her with her coat. He only hesitated for a second, but in that moment the gentleman next to her had finished helping the other person in their group and reached for the redheaded lady's coat to do the same for her. George had lost his chance.

He found out later that her name was Doris Hamilton, that she was visiting her aunt, and that she came from Shropshire. George never saw her again. She became one of several women he sometimes thought of throughout the years, thought of with a kind of distant longing he could not name.

George was pulled out of his thoughts by the sound of approaching footsteps echoing down the corridor from his office. He returned the book to his coat, and as he got back to his desk, he attempted to steel himself against remembering any more of the past.

A few hours later as he made his way home George walked slower than usual, feeling the weight of *Persuasion* in his breast pocket. His inattention to Doris Hamilton twenty-some-odd years ago still weighed on him. He would not flatter himself that she ever thought about him after that night – after all, he was just a bloke who picked up her scarf and who didn't dance with her – but what if that was supposed to be the beginning of his great romance, and he had missed his chance? Meeting at dances, that's all they ever did in Miss Austen's novels. A torn slip of muslin, an offhand remark about someone being tolerable or not and, three hundred pages later, matrimony. He had read and reread those novels for years, but so far they hadn't helped him find his happy ending. Weren't there a hundred different ways of falling in love? The problem was he didn't know any of them.

George was so caught up in his own thoughts that he didn't hear the sirens at first. It was only when he registered the sight of the men and women around him heading for cover that he realised what was happening.

The closest public air raid shelter was just around the corner, and he joined the press of people heading in that direction. In the distance, the familiar buzz of plane engines joined the warning blare of the sirens. George was just steps from the shelter when he noticed a woman in a plain and ill-fitting brown suit pleading with a small boy. The boy was rooted to the spot, fighting off her advances to take his hands and lead him inside. "I won't, I won't," he kept shouting. By this time, mostly everyone was off the streets, and the woman looked to be at her wits' end. George observed all of this, and for the first time in his life he didn't think, he didn't weigh the consequences, he didn't freeze. He lifted the boy into his arms, and with a free hand, guided the woman the remaining way into the shelter just as the doors were shut.

They made their way down the steps and once below, George lowered the boy to the ground. In his bewilderment, the child instinctively reached for the woman's hand. "Thank you, sir," she said to George.

"It was nothing."

The woman seemed to think she owed George some kind of explanation and went on to say, "He's my sister's boy, you see, and I can usually get him to mind me, but he always fusses when the sirens go off." The boy nodded vigorously, and George gestured to an empty seat. The woman sat down, and the boy silently climbed into her lap. George searched in his pockets and pulled out a peppermint for the child.

"You're very kind," said the woman, "Mister... Mister..."

"Howard. George Howard."

"This is Henry. And I'm Nancy."

"You're going to be a brave little soldier from now on, aren't you, Henry?" George said.

Above them came the sounds of explosions, growing louder. The lights flickered, but stayed on. There was an empty seat at the other end of the room, but George remained where he was.

"I'm sure we won't be here for long," he said. An older woman sitting nearby let out a soft grunt in opposition to this statement. She briskly turned the page of the book she was reading.

"Blast," said Nancy suddenly, "my book. We were on our way back from the library. I must have dropped it in all the commotion."

"If you need something to read..." said George, his voice trailing off as he removed the battered copy of *Persuasion* from his coat.

"Now that is astonishing," she said, looking at him and the volume in amazement. "You probably won't believe me, but this is the very book I had taken out of the library."

What followed were two hours of some of the most pleasant

conversation George had ever been fortunate enough to take part in. It started with a lively debate over which novel was their favorite (Nancy expressed a keen partiality to *Emma*), veered into several exchanges of choice quotations, and ended with a fierce defence of Fanny Price on the part of Nancy in her attempt to dissuade George from his notion that the character was dull.

"Was there ever a heroine who knew her own mind better than Fanny?" she said as the all-clear started to sound. By this time, little Henry had fallen asleep, and George, without a word, once again lifted the boy into his arms and accompanied Nancy home. It wasn't a long walk, and George found himself disappointed when they approached a house with a woman waiting in the doorway. It was Nancy's sister, and within seconds, she was fretting and fawning over the sleeping child. She had been worried sick, she said to Nancy, when she returned home and they weren't there. Nancy and her books… They really would be the death of her one day. As the sister took Henry to bed, George and Nancy were left alone in the half-darkened corridor.

"Thank you again for all of your help, Mr Howard. I don't know what I would have done with Henry if you hadn't come along."

"Please don't mention it," he said. "I was only too glad to be of assistance."

"Do you often find yourself rescuing harrowed aunts and their troublesome nephews? I should perhaps call you Captain Wentworth." Her face lit up with a smile.

Without wanting to, he heard himself say, "I must go."

"Of course," Nancy said, flustered. "I don't mean to keep you."

George stepped through the doorway but lingered on the front step, turning back to her. "I believe you'll find the library on Charlotte Street has a much better selection of books. And it has the distinction of possessing its own air raid shelter."

"Thank you, Mr Howard. I will keep that in mind."

"And I promise to take another look at *Mansfield Park*. I hope to stand corrected in my original estimations of Fanny Price."

"Please do, Mr Howard, and tell me what you think." She lowered her eyes, shy suddenly, aware perhaps of what her words implied.

George took a step closer to her and said, "I look forward to it. Next Saturday, perhaps, in the afternoon? We could go for tea. If you'd like."

His words were met by a deep and radiating smile. "That would be lovely."

"Until then," he said. He waited on the step until she closed the front door and then slowly walked out into the night, letting the fog engulf him as he disappeared down the street. For the first time since the evening of that dance so many years ago, though he was uncertain of his fate, he allowed himself to hope.

༄

My inspiration: Last year I realised that I'm now older than all of Jane Austen's heroines. I decided that my story's narrator should be a man who feels he is beyond any hope of romantic attachment but suddenly finds himself inspired by Captain Wentworth. The title comes from a line in *Persuasion*.

LUCKY WICKHAM –
A BLOG FROM AFGHANISTAN

Judith Earnshaw

Lucky Wickham –
A Blog from Afghanistan

Judith Earnshaw

Well, here I am at Camp Bastion. And what a journey, my friends, to get here. They huddled us all like cattle into a cargo plane, where you can sit on the floor or squat, but barely stand. That may be all very well for the rank and file (and some of them are pretty rank), but it's not what you expect for the officer class.

And, having got here, what a destination! Four miles by two of raucous airstrip and shanty buildings set in the desert north of Lashkar Gah. Let me tell you, even if there were not a war here, this is not an area of untapped tourist potential. Sand, sand, sand as far as you can see, apart from the base and the occasional indentation of a wadi. And of course, the pitted roads where the Taliban, as they put it, plant roadside flowers. Well, this is my second deployment and I have seen those flowers burst into bloom, turning the head of a young recruit into an exploding red peony. And I don't intend to put myself in their way. The way I see it, there are plenty of young hotheads who have come out here for the action, and if action is what they want, then let them have it. It's always best to send the kids out in front, because they're faster on their feet anyway. I'm a family man, me, and I've got to think of my own kids back home. I do best bringing up the rearguard.

Not that I intend getting sent out on patrol if I can help it. I didn't train in logistics and IT for those skills to go unused. I'm sure the top brass will see that, and they'll want to keep me back here on base. Besides, I have certain strategic planning skills, and more than one colonel has found it handy to have me at his elbow. I know my place too. I can come up with a sound attack plan and still convince the colonel that it was entirely his own idea and I served no more purpose than a sounding-board. I'm not all about self-aggrandisement. I don't need to patent my thinking. It suits me if I can just do my stuff safely on base, even if you do need ear plugs to fend off the battle of the pumped-up house music and the planes landing and leaving.

Do you know, there's a local farmer here who's planted fields of melons just outside the walls of the camp? He uses the outflowing water from Bastion to irrigate his crop. That's my kind of man. Why waste a resource when you can turn it to your own profit?

When they told us our regiment was being deployed to Helmand, they suggested we might all like to write a will. *Like to?* What a kindly touch. Don't you just love the British Army? Well, my own decision was that I wouldn't do that because I've got sweet FA to leave anyway, and one thing I can be sure of is that the bro-in-law will see Liddy and the kids all right if anything happens to me. To say nothing of the army pension. So I thought, to hell with the will, I'm going to write a blog instead, and here we go. One thing about the army – you may not always be able to get a shower, and sometimes there isn't that much to eat, but you can always find an internet socket. Especially if you're in IT.

One thing I used to think before they first deployed me to the desert was that you would get these big amazing skies. You'd see the stars as clear as though you and they were alone in the universe together. But let me tell you, it's not like that. In the desert the air is full of sand and dust, and the back of your throat gets raw and your nostrils fug up. Most nights you can barely see the stars. And then there's the pollution, and the smell of the petrol and the ordnance, and the heavy equipment chuntering around, destroying any sense of place. It's the fog of war all right. I've seen better stars in Surrey.

Most of the blokes out here do a lot of thinking about their families back home, and to be honest, I do too. There's time to take stock between the spurts of action. And a lot of them – even the officers – seem to swing between the view sentimental and the view pornographic, depending on how the mood takes them. I'm not exempt, though I'm probably less sentimental than some, having always seen myself as a hard-headed realist. You need a bit of that to survive when you're adopted out of an abusive family at the age of two. Still, I can't complain. The bro-in-law's old dad was a proper father to me, and to be honest, I think he liked me better than his own son. More approachable and easy-going you see. Darcy was always a bit up himself and standoffish, even as a kid. We didn't play that well together. I'd say there was some jealousy. I was jealous of what he stood to gain when his old man passed on, and Darcy was always jealous that I could charm the birds out of the trees. And later on charm the birds out of their knickers. That was never Darcy's way. I'd say he was on the verge of being socially autistic, with the crass things he sometimes used to say. Putting girls down *in their earshot*. That was never going to win him friends and influence people. He might as well have posted defamatory comments on Facebook. But I'm getting a bit ahead of myself here.

There goes another plane. If I get out of this deployment with my eardrums intact, it'll be a miracle. Even if I do avoid getting sent out on patrol and having to field the explosions. Because they'll get your ears even if they don't get your guts.

Well, back to my childhood. So long as the old man was alive – and he did live to see me through public school and Sandhurst – things went pretty well for me. I never objected to the army – being an officer does give you quite a cachet – but I was always pretty clear that I didn't intend to get shot. Clear with myself, that is. You don't brag those things around the regiment. But really I think I had quite an attachment to Darcy's old dad. How could you help it? The guy genuinely loved me. So when he keeled over with a heart attack at the tender age of 60, I went all to pieces. That's when all that stuff with my stepsister Georgie came up. I think she was in pieces too and we comforted each other. Maybe a bit too much.

Now look, I know under-age sex is against the law – and obviously for good reasons. I know it doesn't look good when a young man in his twenties has it off with a girl of fourteen. But let's get clear about who was the predator here. Georgie was so up for it, it was embarrassing. She couldn't get enough of me. And she was a big girl for fourteen too. Very well developed. I know I should have been stronger, but the flesh is weak, especially when the testosterone gets pumping.

Well, I did know that Mrs and Darcy wouldn't take it to Court. They'd fight shy of putting the family through that, and Georgie never would have given evidence. Not against me. I think there's still a soft spot there. But they did what they could. Kicked me out without a brass farthing to my name and said they didn't want to see me again. They said, "You've had your education and you're on your own now." They said, "Nature wins out over nurture every time, and you've just reverted to your true colours." They said, "That's the sort of family you came from, and that's the sort of person you are." The old man wouldn't have done that. He'd dropped me plenty of hints he intended to provide for me, which Darcy in his wisdom chose to ignore. And if the guy hadn't died when he did, I really think none of this would have happened. Georgie and I were both a bit beside ourselves with grief.

Shit, I can hear explosions. I think some of the locals are having fun with rocket-propelled grenades. They won't get anywhere; we're much too well-defended in here, but it doesn't make for a peaceful night's sleep. And you'd think they'd be deterred by the fact we've got so many Afghans in here with us: trainees, cooks, interpreters. These people have no loyalty.

Well, after that it was the army. Kosovo, Iraq twice, and now Afghanistan for the second time. But mainly – though I've seen things I shouldn't – I've managed to keep away from the front line. What's even better is that I've kept away from the front line whilst building up my credit and advancing my career. You don't have to be brave to do that. You just have to be clever.

In one way I wasn't so clever though. There's just too much down time in the army. What is it they say: "Four fifths boredom and one fifth sheer terror"? That's about right, I think. And I started filling a bit too much of the down time with internet gaming. Well, gambling I suppose you would say. I always thought I was lucky Wickham, but some of those poker players out on the net are the business. They're professionals and I was just a humble soldier. So I lost my shirt.

That's how it was when I went back on leave one time – nowhere much to go any more, so it was swallow your sorrows in the form of small blue pills and go clubbing. And that's where I met Liddy. Now I had no intention of anything serious coming out of this, though Liddy was hot in the sack, always has been. That made me want to see her again and again. And then Liddy got pregnant.

My view of it was "It happens all the time – you can get rid of it or you can be a single mum, there's no stigma these days. And it's your choice Liddy, I won't influence you." So Liddy decided she'd have the baby, and then it turned out she had this rather posh old-fashioned family, though they didn't have as much money as I would have liked. You'd never have had Liddy down as coming from one of those horsey, county, High Anglican families – she seemed like a right little player. But the family had views. Can you believe it, in this day and age, father actually took me aside and said he thought the right thing to do would be for me to marry Liddy. I have to admit, he seemed a bit embarrassed about it, though not as embarrassed as I was. Well, I thought, I'll come clean. And I'll see if I can cut a deal. I told him about my debts and how I couldn't really support a wife and kid unless someone sorted me out a hundred grand. I'd love to, of course. But I just couldn't give them the life they deserved. I was looking round their country pile all the time thinking, "This is nice, this is really nice." But Dad said he didn't have that sort of money. And then, just as I was walking out of the house, thinking that was it for me and Liddy, I bumped into Darcy.

I think we both felt pretty awkward about it. I went red and he went pale. But it turned out Darcy was courting Liddy's elder sister. And knowing, as I do, that the bloke inherited money that should have been mine, and that he's also trebled his fortune at the expense of all good people by working as an investment banker, I thought – there could still be a chance here. There wouldn't be a chance with Darcy himself, of course. As far as he's concerned, implacable resentment is the name of the game. But I got Liddy to introduce me to her sister Lizzy, and boy, did I turn on the charm. I had Lizzy eating out of my hand. I did think, "You'd better watch what's yours, Darcy, or we're going to see a change of ownership here." But what happened was, once Lizzy was on our side, she managed to talk Darcy round. He paid my debts – peanuts to him of course – and Liddy and I got wed.

I didn't think I wanted to marry Liddy, but to be honest, I don't mind. We don't spend that much time together because I'm mostly deployed, but when I go home, Liddy really knows how to give a man a warm welcome. So we've got three kids now and another on the way. That can almost cause a little swell of sentiment.

Oh God no, someone's hammering at my door. My commanding officer. Shit. He thinks that after the grenades the locals sent over last night, we need to send a patrol out before first light and sort them out. And who's the lucky sod who gets to lead the patrol? Yes, Wickham, that'll be you.

One thing about being on base so much is you get the chance to sort yourself out the best possible kit. My flak jacket is second to none. And I'll take up my usual post, covering the rear of the patrol. I really have too much value for the regiment to be expendable. Listen, readers, I'll see you later. It's not for nothing they call me "lucky" Wickham.

❧

My inspiration: I wanted to see whether it would be possible to set the outline of a Jane Austen novel in the very modern world. Wickham is presented as potentially a modern character, to whom it would be easy to allocate a place and a role – and I had read a few blogs from Afghanistan.

BLUE LIAS

Sarah Barr

Blue Lias

ॐ

Sarah Barr

"You can't go back, Annie," Caroline said. "Well, of course you *can*," she qualified in her pedantic way, "but—"

Her dark hair had frizzed up around her face and raindrops fell onto the table as she spoke.

"It wouldn't work," I said.

She nodded vigorously and picked up the ammonite we'd just purchased at the museum. "Don't look back. Don't get stuck in the past."

She was trying to help me.

I understood perfectly why Caroline had been so lucky in love. Although not exactly pretty, she had a friendly appearance, was honest and loyal, and she knew her own mind. What more could any man want? I envied her life even though mine probably seemed fine to outsiders.

The kids I taught probably thought I was already a fossil, a dinosaur, at thirty-one years old.

We gazed out at the rain lashing down the café windows. We'd had to abandon our walk along the sea-front. I wanted to treat her to tea and cakes before we went back to her tiny cottage crammed with babies and a husband who worked from home with varying success.

"Coming here, driving down the narrow main street, seeing the Cobb… it hit me worse than I thought it would." Over the years I'd been careful never to return, even though I only lived in Somerset.

She murmured something sympathetic. "You don't have to go. You could get back into your car and drive home. It's only a college reunion, not an invitation to Buckingham Palace."

"If you hadn't told me he'd be there," I moaned, thinking *I'm fatter, older, a primary school teacher, and have nothing of any interest whatsoever to talk about whereas he—*

"You look great," she said firmly. "Your new haircut really emphasises your cheekbones and your lovely green eyes."

The reason she'd been lucky in love was because she knew herself, knew who would suit her, and she had gone for him. She had not been deflected.

"You can't have been really right for each other," she said, "or you would have found a way. Don't worry. There's somebody out there for you. Maybe, tonight…"

It was June. We'd finished our exams and come on an end of year outing to a shingle beach at Lyme Regis. There were seven of us including Caroline and Danny – my new gorgeous boyfriend.

We'd met when we'd been on opposite sides of a debate about love, that hackneyed proposition that it was better to have loved and lost than never to have… well you know it, and you can imagine the points that were made by a roomful of nineteen and twenty year olds.

I was too shy in those days to say more than a couple of sentences and I only made myself do it because I wanted to be a teacher and I reckoned I had to get used to public speaking.

Dan and I walked around the sloping beach, collecting driftwood and dried seaweed, piling it up into a great bonfire. Caro and the others unwrapped sausages, chopped salad, buttered bread, opened bottles and propped them upright with large stones. Then they wandered about looking for fossils, tapping with a hammer that someone had brought, their calls and laughter reflecting the relief that exams were over and the holidays beginning.

"What sort of grades do you think you'll get?" I asked Dan as we lit the fire and stood with our arms round each other.

"I don't care about my results," he said, which surprised me because I thought he was ambitious. "I do care about you, Annie."

Our relationship had galloped along after that first meeting – as can happen when two young people spend a large part of every day and night together, even revising at the same table in the library – and we'd hardly argued about anything since that first debate.

I envisaged a final year much the same and then moving in together as we started our first jobs, our first year of real independence. We loved each other; we were twin stars, two halves of a whole.

"I've got something to ask you," he said, heaving another boulder to form an edge to the fire, "something important." He raked both hands through his vivid red hair. I held my breath. The sea made a distant lapping swish, and seagulls cried their messages.

"I'm leaving uni. I'm sorry. I've decided to go to Oz. Hitch up with Dad."

"Your Dad? Australia? You haven't seen him for years." I heard sobs rise up in my throat.

"I know, but I want to make my way in the world, not study books, geography. I can do real geography, look after the land and earn at the same time. He's got me a job on his farm."

"You have a great opportunity to get a degree, better yourself, but you can't hack it, can you, Daniel?" That sounded so like my snobby parents. "Sorry. It's just..." I swallowed hard. "...so unexpected."

"Annie, I want you to come with me," he continued, his voice intense. "We could get married, we're old enough. I want us to emigrate. Together. I want to make a life for us. Please."

"Married? I'm not ready for that. And what about my music degree?"

He knew I found home life difficult. He probably thought I'd jump at the opportunity. Once I'd got over the shock, I did. I agreed to go with him.

"What happened then, in a nutshell?" Caro asked as we walked back along the promenade. "Why did you guys split up?"

She'd played her part in all that. Didn't she remember the lecture she'd given me about valuing myself, not chasing after a man?

I noticed the Victorian-style street lamps, black against the pink sky, their shaded lights hanging from curled metal ammonites. The evening air was chilly, damp. The weak sun glinted over the sea and on the rocks, the blue lias of the distant cliff, picking out the layers and layers of time.

It was all right for her. She hadn't been faced with the conflict of having to choose between family and boyfriend.

"In a nutshell..." I said, and had an immediate image of Danny pulling down a branch, showing me the cluster of hazelnuts with glossy shells, perfect and strong. I remembered our argument and the bad way we'd parted. "My parents were dead against the idea. Said we were too young. Wanted me to continue with my degree – that was important to them. Plus, they didn't really like him, they thought he came from the wrong sort of family, and Dad has always had a thing against people with red hair. In the end, I gave in."

We turned the corner to Fisherman's Cottage. "I must just warn you," she said, "Hugo is pretty depressed about losing his job. But we're OK."

*

"I'd like to do a boat-building apprenticeship," her husband explained, "but with all the unemployment round here, who's going to take me on?" We'd put the children to bed and now Caro was reading them a story.

He handed me a glass of the red wine I'd brought. "Great to see you. Here's to life, love and... work."

I thought about Dan, how concerned he'd been about finding work and earning a living, and how lacking in understanding I had been.

"Are you still playing the piano?" Hugo asked.

I told him how my music hadn't flourished, how I'd got my teaching qualification belatedly and how I liked the children but not the admin, the usual sort of teachers' complaint.

"And what about your man?"

"What man?"

"I can't remember his name – isn't he in an orchestra? Why didn't you bring him along?"

I muttered something about that relationship being over.

"Time to go," Caro said, ushering the babysitter into the living-room and whispering, "They're asleep – but here's our mobile number."

"I can't understand why Danny has come from the other side of the world for this reunion," Hugo continued as the three of us climbed the steps to the Bay View Hotel where the party was taking place. "Unless it's because he wants to see you, Annie."

"Didn't I tell you?" Caro replied. "His email said he was coming over here anyway, for a wedding. For all we know, it could be his own."

"Why didn't you tell me that when we were in the café?" I snapped, angry, not just with her, but also with myself. I had no right to expect him to be single.

"Because you'd have gone home, Annie, and I didn't want you to." She squeezed my hand. "Don't think too badly of me."

It was a decade since he'd left. Australia had seemed such a distant place to me then, somewhere I knew little about. I'd learned more in the intervening years from Aussies who were over here teaching or working in bars. But I'd never been there myself. Images of drought, floods and wildfires were graphic reminders of the extremes of nature. A farmer out there would need to focus on the essentials in life, I thought, not fuss on about what might have been.

Not a word had been exchanged between us since that last weekend when I'd told him that I was going to do what my parents wanted and continue at Exeter, get my degree. That I wasn't going with him. He hadn't contacted me once he arrived, not an email, not even a Christmas card. I got a few snippets of information from friends but eventually these dried up. He blanked me as if I'd never existed. I had thought we felt the same about each other, but I'd been wrong. I was too hurt to get in touch with him.

"It was never really serious, Hugo," I explained as we stood looking out through the picture-window at the expanse of sea, the dark walls of the Cobb, a few lights here and there, fishing boats setting out. What was I saying? This was a man I'd briefly been tempted to marry. "He came from a wealthy background, and my father liked him. But I knew that wasn't enough."

I couldn't settle for second best after what I'd had with Dan… Dan who I could now see over on the other side of the room, talking to people he seemed to know. He wasn't as tanned as I expected. Slim, tall. My heart lurched and pounded. Don't, I warned myself. You're an adult now. Calm down.

"Caro and I were sorry to hear about your mother," Hugo said.

"Yes, it was horrible. I guess I needed a shoulder to cry on, and he was around. That's probably why the relationship went on, but it's all over now." *If Dan had stayed, if he hadn't abandoned me...*

I stopped, took a deep breath. The last thing I wanted was to burst into tears at this reunion. I really did need to put the past behind me. "I'm sorry, that sounded awful. I'm so angry with myself. Why didn't I trust my own judgement? It's not as if I've achieved anything in the last decade. With hindsight, I should have made a different decision and gone with Dan to Australia."

"You put your life on hold for years, to care for your mum," Hugo said, giving me a hug. "What could be a better use of time than that? And by all accounts she wasn't the easiest person to nurse."

It was a relief to unburden myself to Hugo. Perhaps it was easier with him than with Caro because he had suffered his own reversals. "There's never been anyone else for me since Danny," I said. "No one. But he won't understand that. He's a man. Men are pragmatic." I nearly said arrogant.

"Whoa!" Hugo held his hand up. "You can't speak for all men like that."

I'd been so caught up in my own emotions that I hadn't seen Dan coming towards us. His eyes were burning into me. I couldn't look at him. Hugo slipped away through a group of people.

"I heard what you just said." His voice had that familiar intensity and also, now, an Australian twang. "It shocked me."

I couldn't reply. Would it be a mistake to say I regretted my early, youthful decision? Don't look back. Don't get stuck in the past. Move on.

"I couldn't stay angry for all that time," he said. "But when I stopped, you'd found someone else."

"You made your decision to go!" I hit back. "Didn't discuss it with me first. Why didn't you wait? What about my plans?"

He stared into his pint, as if trying to spot something very precious at the bottom of the glass. "I guess I was young. And broke. And very foolish. I'm sorry for it. I've been pretty lonely as a result, you may be glad to know."

I felt a rush of forgiveness that was completely unexpected, also a sense of shame as I recalled my own harsh words to him before he went. And then I wanted to laugh out loud. It was so wonderful to see him again.

"I'm sorry, Dan. But I was young, too, and thought I was doing the sensible thing. Even though..." But I didn't want to get in to the whole thing about my parents' unhappy marriage. "Aren't you getting married yourself, soon?"

"What? Me? No! My sister is." He looked embarrassed, but continued firmly. "What you decided wasn't wrong. If you'd come with me then, you wouldn't have been here for your mum. D'you know, you were always a very kind person, Anne. That was a quality I loved in you."

Loved. Not love. "I heard you've done well and have your own farm." I hoped that sounded generous, not envious. "We mustn't look back or get stuck in the past," I said, to protect my feelings.

"We're not getting stuck. Or shall I say, I'm not. We're different now," he said.

We were the same, though, in so many ways. I would never forget what a brilliant time we'd had together as a young couple. My first love would always be completely special to me. We were who we were today because of the past. And so I wouldn't change things, even if I could. Like the layers of blue lias in the cliff, one era was always built on the previous one.

And now we must trust that something good will come of what we've been through. We try not to beat ourselves up about the past and hope we'll be able to work out a way of being together.

❧

My inspiration: My story has a contemporary setting and is inspired by the character of Anne Elliot in *Persuasion*. I have used the subject of separation from love and the influence of family and friends in causing this. My story is also about the passage of time and how people may change as they grow older. I have used the setting Lyme Regis as this is also important in *Persuasion*, and have also reworked other ideas in the novel e.g. the symbol of the hazelnut.

KATIE

Susan Piper

Katie

Susan Piper

"Old witch!" she said. I am sure that was what the girl muttered as she left the room, taking away the unwanted tray. So I am a witch am I – a witch because I had the audacity to give an instruction to a maid? A witch because everyone is intent on ignoring me now that I have been forced to take to my bed? They need to learn that while my heart may be weak, made thin and flat by the pounding hammers of duty and disappointment, my hearing is as keen as ever.

I have been *"My Lady"*, delivered with bowed head, *"Lady Catherine de Bourgh"*, in clarion tones from liveried footmen and *"Mama,"* whispered with soft affection, and now I am *"old witch"* because I am confined to this room, alone. I am a motionless, easy target. I am blanketed with ingratitude, nursed with ignorance and physicked with insolence. Breathe Catherine, sink deeper in your pillows and do not let yourself be roused. Your heart will not stand it! Surely it is enough to have to die alone without having to suffer name-calling and brattish behaviour.

In my half-sleep just now I caught sight of the booted leg of someone just leaving the room – who was that? Maybe my nephew came to see me again and went away when he thought I was sleeping. No. The leg I saw belongs to a younger man. My nephew is past middle age now, heavier. And he has already been to do his duty, to pay his last respects. With the wife. Elizabeth.

My child, my Anne, did not spend a single one of her last hours alone. I held the skeletal hand and bathed the chalky forehead with eau de cologne. No words were necessary. My girl slipped away safe in the knowledge that her mother was there. The mother who she knew had never forgiven herself for failing to secure for her daughter the future she deserved. I could hardly make out her final, whispered words, as even at that last minute she tried to comfort me. *Don't be too disappointed, Mama. I was never you. I was never disappointed.*

How many hours have passed? I am aware of comings and goings – familiar shadows, professional and uniformed, slip in and out of my perception, doing their job without regard or affection. More blankets have been pressed upon me but I can't stir myself to tell them to stop, that I am being smothered! All I want is to sink into sleep without weight or trouble! All my life I have had to carry such a burden of responsibility – a solitary responsibility!

I listened to their children on the lawn while we exchanged pleasantries. Just how many have they produced? But no, that must have been an earlier visit. Their offspring must be quite grown up now, long past playing sailors and flying kites. Elizabeth has hardly aged a day while my girl has withered and disappeared. Elizabeth kept her eyes lowered, whether through shame or to hide her distaste I don't know. She was a good girl, intelligent and pretty, and I loved every minute of her visits – such feist and fury and forthrightness! The days she spent here as a guest were bright and lively. She will never know that I was on the point of offering her a position in my house. She will never know how rarely such an offer is made. But the girl gave her heart in error. She put her heart in a place reserved for another – and manipulated her position as a guest in my world to do it.

And despite Elizabeth Darcy's transgressions, when she takes to her bed one day she will be surrounded by children and grandchildren, not alone with servants calling her names, while I who only ever tried to do things properly am left alone! Years of negotiation and expectation ruined. What a power my Rosings and his Pemberley would have created together! And Darcy – how could my daughter have failed to thrive with Darcy at her side? Darcy with his laughing hazel eyes and mahogany hair – such intelligence and humour would, I am sure, have given her the strength and resilience she lacked all her life.

I hate this dozing in and out of wakefulness. Now here I lie with tears on my face. This is humiliating. Compose yourself, Catherine. How I hate what I have become.

I had a chance for that kind of love.

But laughing hazel eyes and mahogany hair would not secure me a future. Papa had explained that. Futures were built on land and estates and money.

I was so complimented that Papa confided in me. It turned out that there was a past to pave over as well as a future to build. He explained patiently that he had invested heavily in my sister and me. Had we ever wanted for anything? Had any privilege ever been denied us? The answer to both questions was, of course, "no". That investment had been made so that we could be assured of a secure and dignified future but it had been at a price. Now it was time for that investment to be repaid.

I understood. I knew that Papa would not have to confide in my sister. My sister had already begun to repay the investment that had been made in her. If I felt bitter it was only because she had found golden hair and a handsome figure to go with her solid future. It didn't take so many tears to wash away the bitterness. My sister was so generous of spirit, never gloating and her pity for what I gave up was pure and sincere. The proof of this was the constant reminders she gave of our promise. She vowed that even though my horizon had changed direction since it was made, the promise we gave in the frivolous daydreams of first love would be kept in any event.

There had never been a formal promise to my green eyes and mahogany hair. But I still felt obliged to write to my disappointed suitor and thank him for his compliments and society, and to express my hopes that our paths would cross in the future. He did not answer and further correspondence was returned unopened.

I gained a husband of my father's choosing. I gained a frail, quiet man who lived to see his only daughter born but not much longer. An unfair bargain – because he gained me. As Lady Catherine de Bourgh, I began the task of moulding myself into the guardian of Rosings, becoming my husband's right hand. My husband gained a woman who commanded respect. I learned to listen. Every whisper and call was information I might one day need as I made Rosings one of the most desirable estates in the south. I delivered what my father needed from me.

I am taken with such fits of trembling, a sensation that I have rarely been prey to other than in anger. It must be a fever for I am consumed with heat. Swaddled like a baby to cause them less trouble.

I never looked into those laughing eyes again but I read about him from time to time. He made an embarrassing spectacle of himself for some months – he revealed a terrible weakness for drink. I tormented myself with the thought that I might be responsible for this, but my sister convinced me that I flattered myself. Fortunately for him, his attractiveness and amenable nature meant he had good and true friends around him. The last time I saw his name I read that he had invested very well and had made himself at home in Virginia. I sometimes wonder if he enjoyed as good a return on his investment as my dear Papa did. I cannot believe he could have.

Just now I dreamed that I was being held. I dreamed that I leaned again into that shoulder, my face in his shirt and his arms around me and felt myself tremble from head to toe. As I stood in his arms, shaking, I felt vast skies open up above us, and the future was a horizon that we would move towards together. We stood in the arbour, unseen from my father's house, and I trembled at the chance I was taking and so much more. I shivered with an excitement that I didn't understand but I felt that as long as I was held by those arms I could face any adventure. I woke to find that instead of arms, it is these covers that hold me. I know my mind is fretful and over-excited, but I feel that I am being borne down upon, not just by covers but by furnishings, panelling, bricks and mortar – all the things that I have chosen and arranged so carefully, and now they push the very breath out of my lungs.

At least there is some compassion in this house. Just outside wakefulness, someone has been kind enough to stroke away the humiliating tears.

We were the toast of the town, the year we came out! My sister, being but ten months my senior, shared my first season with me and I could not have asked for a better, more light-hearted – or discrete – companion. Our colouring, our gowns and our moods all complimented each other.

As these long days pass, I take up less and less of the bed. Now I scarcely raise a ripple under the heavy counterpane. All the energy I had as a young girl – dancing until dawn and then staying up for hours retelling every enchanting moment of the night with friends and my sister. And late one night my sister and I clasped hands and crossed our hearts, promising that when we had children – never a doubt that one would have a boy and the other a girl – they would marry.

Except for a taste of music on the breeze, it has all evaporated. Even that ultimate promise, that solemn agreement was swept away. When Elizabeth convinced Darcy to dissolve his ties with my daughter, the last vestige of my youth and innocence melted away.

These memories are too exuberant! They make my breath almost impossible to draw. Sure enough here is the doctor. He holds my wrist, gently making sure my heart still beats! But who is holding my other hand? Smooth strong fingers hold mine quiet on the cover. I will remember quieter times in the hope that my heart does not feel the strain too much. I want these covers off. I want to feel the breeze.

I want to feel the breeze through the window like I did when he came to call some days after the dance. The delicate curtains were set fluttering. Fingers brushed while passing a teacup. He would have been enough for me, Papa. I didn't need any more.

It gets dark earlier and earlier. The windows are closed and curtains drawn only a few hours after lunch. This room is so close and still. I must call out! Please someone take off these accursed coverings! Push the curtains aside and throw open the windows! Thank you, thank you! Yes! At last some air and I can move my arms and legs – I could almost dance again. *Thank you so much – you can call me a witch if you want and anything else besides but please don't close the windows again! Yes I heard but it doesn't matter. No don't cry – it doesn't matter. Please don't shut me in anymore! Who is that at the door, smoothing his hair and tugging his coat? No matter...*

Who will I be now? I am no more the mother, no more the Lady – not even the witch.

The breeze is gentle, solicitous. No lifting or blush-causing, just a cool and musical breeze blowing over me. The breeze is interrupted by a figure passing the window. I don't need to open my eyes. I know who my visitor is. I think I have known all along who has been hovering, finally coming to find me. I feel his head lower onto the pillow beside me. The breeze carries blossom and birdsong, bells and ballrooms. It is not the breeze, it is his breath, replacing mine as I wait for him to speak. Finally.

"Katie."

❦

My inspiration: A cynical view would be that heroes are people who do what we agree with, while a villain is somebody who gets in our way. Maybe heroes are born but I think that villains rarely are. They are shaped. I have tried to write a story about the shaping of a villain, giving her a chance to show how she didn't start out that way. In fact, it's possible that she had a great deal in common with the heroine of Jane Austen's story. I started with the villain and worked backwards.

WIKRAM

Sulaxana Hippisley

Wikram

ॐ

Sulaxana Hippisley

'Mr Wickham was the happy man towards whom almost every
female eye was turned…'

Seated on a stone wall overlooking the bay, Wikram Jayanath was
assured at once of his own talents. His suspicions had been roused
by the first glance, but a second more furtive look confirmed what
his heart felt and his eyes could no longer see. It did not escape
his attention that the subject of his gaze was dressed in a most
unbecoming pink polyester shalwar kameez, and that her gaunt
neck, even with an abundance of gold chokers, would not be viewed
favourably by prospective mothers-in-law. Her buxom companion,
greedily occupied with a paper bag of jalebi, did not present much
of an improvement. Yet, desperate times could persuade him to
overlook such minor indiscretions. Of course, no self-respecting
Brahmin girl would expect to secure a match on Juhu beach and in
such a manner.

Wikram was well acquainted with the near impossible task in
this day and age of assessing the dowries of young women purely
on account of their dress. The girls from the slums could wander all
over town clad in counterfeit Versace jeans and sunglasses, virtually

undetectable amongst the dotcom heiresses. The intimate plans he had once so easily executed concerning particular ladies at Deewali, Navaratri or at the nuptials of distant cousins were now of little use to him. Following his own hasty marriage to the youngest Banerjee daughter, Lalitha, Wikram noted that his invitations to the annual round of Mumbai social gatherings had ceased to arrive that year. Still, his present difficulties could not be forgotten in the name of vanity, and Wikram proceeded to clear his throat and continue with the new course of action designed for this very purpose. This consisted of berating a non-existent employee on his mobile phone, within audible distance from the ladies in question. "Of course, damn fool, the Nikkei was going to fall today, did I not tell you to purchase those stocks earlier? Get me Shivanathan on 2566!."

A few passing children and a haggard rubbish collector on the promenade paused to gaze in envy at the heady exploits of the businessman. *Success*. Yet his prime audience, the young women, were now little more than colourful dots on the horizon.

Not yet married twelve months, Wikram Jayanath, being a man of the world, knew that his wife and her family could not be counted upon to provide an adequate income of any kind. There was only one source, one person from which such an assurance could come. It pained him to look upon the white card with the ornate silver script that Lalitha had deposited so carefully in his blazer pocket that morning. But there it was. "Darshan industries - pursuing excellence in every way. Firdous Darshan. Chief Executive Officer." As Wikram stood on the pavement to peruse the card, the towering thirty-six floor monolith behind him bore the very same logo of a large "D" entwined within a silver coronet. Any inhabitant of Mumbai would instantly recognise the logo and it could be seen on various billboards, on the plastic awnings above markets, or on the silver cards that enabled you to withdraw money conveniently.

It would be presumptuous to describe Wikram's near thirty years of acquaintance with Darshan as cordial or even amiable. Yet Darshan – childhood friend, companion, master and now reluctant brother-in-law, by way of Wikram's ill-made match – was a continuous presence at every precarious twist and turn in his life. With few connections and even fewer virtues to his own name, Wikram knew that a lesser man would not have presided over his elopement with as much dignity and grace as Darshan had done. Perhaps it was a misplaced sense of duty that had compelled Darshan to recruit the services of his friend, the district registrar, to carry out the deed and to pay off a large portion of Wikram's debts. All matters aside, no one could deny that they were kin once again since Darshan had wed the second eldest of the Bannerjee daughters, Leela.

He resolved to tell Lalitha that he had visited Darshan with the very intention of requesting a private audience, but had found him otherwise occupied.

"Wikram, we are so lucky, lucky, lucky to know Darshan Ji, aren't we?" Lalitha had said that morning, running a plastic comb through her wet tresses. "You're practically brothers now and Leela said he would not rest until he had found you something. So nice of him to offer, even after all his help with our wedding!"

He had nodded. Pity the poor girl, how could she possibly know about his battles with Darshan that had begun in infancy. Destiny had bound them together again, yet she knew little about what it meant for one man to push a begging bowl before another in the prime of his life. To prostrate himself before Firdous Darshan in the manner of a pilgrim at the foot of a mandir, when they had sipped from the same tin cup, slept in the same hammock and sat upon each other's shoulders to reach the mangoes on the high branches. It would not do. This much he knew as he made his way home to their lodgings in the ramparts of town.

Upon reaching the green-fronted guesthouse, he hurried up the narrow staircase, taking great care to avoid another unfortunate encounter with the landlady. The violent clatter of aluminium pots and Malayalam expletives announced another brawl between the couple from Tamil Nadu who resided upstairs. There was no doubt that conjugal bliss was in short supply in the building. As Wikram anticipated, he discovered his wife sprawled across the bed as the result of an industrious afternoon, eyes firmly locked on a silver television transmitting a romantic lament of some kind or another. Seeing him enter the room, she beckoned him to her side. "Oh my Wicky, look at your face, not at all the face I like. Is Mr Darshan working you too hard? He's so moody isn't he? If I meet him again, I'll teach him a thing or two. Oh my Wicky, I am so proud of you!" With this, Lalitha showered her beloved's face with violent kisses and then proceeded to wrap her green voile sari around his dear face. "You make a pretty lady, you do, my Wicky: who can tell that you are my husband when you look so pretty in a sari!"

Wikram had known the flattery of such eighteen year olds before; he had humoured sixteen year olds with flat feet and offered elocution to the occasional fifteen-year-old Brahmin beauty when the occasion presented itself. But to be cajoled thus, to have one's name so disparaged in the act of possession was an offence too far. *My Wicky.* From this, Wikram deduced that his wife's continuous use of the possessive pronoun could only serve to annihilate his former self, his past achievements and what little he had in the name of acquaintances. He pulled her close then, hoping to recover some unspoken mystery from their courtship, but found none. Instead, he saw the tepid pools of her eyes filling with hunger and expectation.

A little after eight that evening came the familiar knock on the door. Mrs Gupta, the landlady, was not accustomed to lodgers who were less than timely with their rent. Wikram had witnessed with his own eyes the measures she took to dispatch unwanted guests along with their meagre possessions. One of which included employing the services of a former boxer by the name of Jyoti who frequented the gambling den opposite the guesthouse. "So, Mr Wikram, I was hoping you might be here." Mrs Gupta smiled. "Late again this month I see. Your wife tells me you have a relative in town, some bigwig CEO that owns the company you work for?"

"Well, relative might be stretching it a little."

"I'm sure your wife isn't mistaken, Mr Wikram. Brother-in-law I think she said."

"We're not very close. Not close at all."

"Oh, well. Mr Wikram, you're a good man and I take it that you understand that this establishment is not to be treated as a halfway house between your village and the street."

"Of course. Mrs Gupta. I'll see that we are clear. Tomorrow."

Whilst Lalitha dozed beside him, Wikram could not find respite in sleep that long night. Words from long ago returned to him and hovered above the canopy of the mosquito net. Darshan. Forthright. Single. CEO. Brahmin. Catch. He had heard the words often enough, mostly being uttered by some covetous matron on the first night of Navaratri when the best matches were being hastily arranged. Wikram added some of his own to the growing list. Immune to the beat of dhol drums, left-footed and humourless. But who could guess that Darshan would conquer the only woman who had shown him nothing but contempt? Leela Banerjee.

Those kohl-lined eyes had turned upon Wikram too that Navaratri. With Darshan hovering on the horizon, he had found an unexpected accomplice in the quick-witted, beady-eyed Leela Banerjee. A woman who was far more than his equal in every measure. A woman who could see through the entire Firdous Darshan facade with little difficulty. Whilst Darshan had looked morose above the throbbing crowd and muttered despondently into his mobile phone, Wikram and Leela had clinked cola bottles and tapped their Garba sticks in great arcs above their heads. Here was a woman whose judgement was not impaired by an excess of Zee TV soaps, the gyrating hips of Bollywood male leads or the affectations held by so many "finishing school" girls. Later, hearing of his misfortunes at Darshan's hand, she had said what he had longed to hear others say of his former friend. "I always thought that Firdous Darshan was capable of really terrible things." Of course, there had been no necessity to impart the whole truth to her. Even so, he had been moved by her willingness to stand on the moth-ridden veranda all evening and hear of his humble beginnings in the Darshan household. And now she was the honourable Mrs Darshan. It was done. "Bhabi," he reminded himself. Dear sweet sister-in-law. Long gone were the knowing exchanges between them. Next year, if he and Lalitha were fortunate enough to be invited to the ancestral house again for Deewali, they would light oil lamps together and nudge each other playfully like long lost brothers and sisters.

Though Wikram knew that Darshan would never receive him in his own offices, he stood at the entrance to Darshan Industries again the following morning. There was no doubt that the opportunity had been engineered by Leela on the account of her long-suffering sister, whose fate was now tied up with the legacy of his misfortunes. Yet he was not without hope. Having attended to his attire with extra care, he wore a fine cotton shirt and the cufflinks that had belonged to his late father. In his hands he held a small red box decorated with colourful garlands. A customary gesture of goodwill towards newlyweds. Why after all this did he feel a sudden tightening of the shoulders and a dryness in his mouth? Who else but Darshan knew the full extent of his capabilities in every endeavour whether good or bad? He had no curriculum vitae to recommend him and no documents headed with the insignia of old Mumbai wealth. Yet Darshan was the only person who could read and comprehend his history, his downfall and his yearning to rise without the need for such formalities. No more wandering. It would of course require a slight biting of the tongue and a surrender of the old ways. A regular income would not only give him the means to provide a home, a maid and a driver for Lalitha, but it would afford him a little of that peace which had proved to be indispensable in his former life.

It was beyond his comprehension how, moments later, he found himself again on the sea front. The contents of the garlanded box lay discarded amidst a pile of rapidly accumulating garbage a few feet away. He drew the card from his pocket for the last time and watched its tiny shreds falling like snow on to the burning sand. But it was not a wasted day after all, for there, on the lone bench overlooking the sea, sat weeping a young woman of no more than sixteen. About her feet lay a selection of enamel-coloured shopping bags, bearing the names of various luxury boutiques. Unaccompanied and without a chaperone in broad daylight, her face told the familiar story of a closeted adolescence in some private girls' school and a single act of rebellion which had led her to the beach that day. She was fortunate, of course, to find such company in a time of distress. Without any further hesitation, he placed the mobile phone under his ear. "The premiere is this evening; I know Mr Khan has rung personally to invite me, but I cannot come alone. I can't disappoint Mr Khan, he's asked for a new actress and I haven't found one." The girl turned. Every eye in the room. Unmistakeable.

৵C

My inspiration: My story was inspired by a moment in *Pride and Prejudice* when, upon entering a room, the eye of every woman present turns to Mr Wickham. I wanted to explore the impact of this gaze upon Wickham following his marriage to Lydia. Setting the story in contemporary India was a deliberate decision, as I believe that the issues Austen raises about marriageability and social status are prevalent in many South Asian societies.

LITTLE ELEGANT COMPLIMENTS

Jacqueline Jean Barrios

Little Elegant Compliments

ℰ

Jacqueline Jean Barrios

"'They arise chiefly from what is passing at the time, and though I sometimes amuse myself with suggesting and arranging such little elegant compliments as may be adapted to ordinary occasions, I always wish to give them as unstudied an air as possible.'" *(Mr Collins,* Pride and Prejudice*)*

In the beginning of the new year of their twelfth year of marriage, Charlotte realised that she looked forward to planning for the hours when Colin came home late, or when he needed to sleep and she knew she would be wide awake. She read *A Hundred Years of Solitude*, the one with the cover bright with flowers, or *Anna Karenina* with the purple hydrangeas. She drank a chilled bottle of the good Chablis or, if it was one of those nights, a short squat tumbler of Maker's Mark Bourbon with the red wax seal. She ate guava jam tarts.

Such was the evening ritual. The hours, once a colourless wasteland, needed activity to soften the corners. They were filled with self-observation and waiting. The time, still and disquieting, also contained moments where she caught herself losing her footing somehow, or visited by the worry that she was forgetting something very important.

Her husband Colin, sensitive to the temperature and the gas

bills, referred to her body as a furnace, her body quietly heating up as she slept. He needed curtains, quiet drifting, a thin coverlet, even temperatures, and no longer found her bedside reading soothing or sultry.

Tonight at 3 a.m., with no school tomorrow, she knew sleep would not come. She felt the bedclothes become stale around her. She rose, and feeling for the door in the dark, glanced at the rising and falling of her husband's chest.

Downstairs, there was still a blanket on the couch from the previous two nights, and Marquez lay in the basket at the foot of the bookshelf. She felt the draft fluttering the curtains. Colin had forgotten to close the sliding door; he had insisted she demonstrate she knew how to lock and unlock it during the first week after they moved in. In those early months, she often forgot her keys and wished to leave the door open, just in case. He was horrified. He was adamant that she should lock the doors and double check them, just in case. She went out towards the glass panels, clicked down the lock, pushed the door closed. She gave it a pull and felt the resistance.

Just outside the sliding door could have been a garden. Unit 27, 1500 Pasadena Street was a cement-bound condominium with a walled-in patio that she once imagined she would fill with growing things. The first thing Colin wanted to do was buy screens, beautiful sunburst-patterned rattan screens, for the balcony. He bought duct tape for the spaces in between. An afternoon was spent contemplating the angles from which the neighbours could potentially glimpse their fully-clothed bodies.

Charlotte's thoughts went to Colin's meticulousness about clothes, always insisting on her having both shirt and underwear on while walking around the house. As for Colin, he would fully tuck in his undershirt into his pants and belt, shave, then undo the whole pant-and-belt ensemble when he was ready to put on his dress shirt.

His row of freshly laundered shirts satisfied him and pleased her. Charlotte, who taught English, once took a picture to show her class, as it reminded her of the scene in *The Great Gatsby* where Daisy sobs at Gatsby's shirts. *Shirts with stripes and scrolls and plaids in coral and apple green and lavender and faint orange with monograms of Indian blue.* Charlotte enjoyed the uniformity and the colors, the patterns, the labels inside. She regularly arranged the collar stays she found littered about the floor. She had certain favourites: the silver Nordstrom ones, the hard black plastic ones from Ralph Lauren, the bright orange ones with the figure of the naked woman.

Colin had never finished the book, though he took great care in picking out the best hardbound copy and leaving it in his briefcase, conspicuous enough so his clients could see. Charlotte felt his pleasure at her literary leanings. He frequently borrowed her observations and recommendations, repeating them in casual conversations meant to impress, or to imply a well-read intellectualism whilst sipping boutique coffee in Los Feliz cafes or eating hundred-dollar lunches at Patina or Spago.

The bergamot (*...our authentic Earl Grey uses finest quality black China Congou leaf blended with the essential oils of the bergamot fruit, which has a fresh, citrus flavour...use a warmed teapot and add one teaspoon of tea per person and an extra 'one for the pot'...*) from earlier that evening perfumed the space, and Charlotte – awake, solitary – read her book with half a mind on Marquez, and the other half held in suspense, waiting for sleep. She thought of tea, the famous 'Sabah' tea her parents would make for guests during her childhood in Kota Kinabalu on the island of Borneo. Tea, despite the heat – as the ceilings hummed with the sound of whirring fans like prehistoric dragonflies, dipping and casting shadows through transparent wings. She remembered her mother's Evian spray bottles, dewing faces and necks. This made her think of the conservatory she had recently visited at the

Huntington Botanical Gardens. The rainforest garden re-created a cool humidity that transported her back as she wandered beneath the mist that fizzed out from nozzles every few minutes. Inside the vast Victorian space of iron facets tracing the sky in radial designs, she followed the spiral of the path shaded by the elegant arm of a banana or climbing vines of passion fruit. At the bottom she looped around to observe the underside of the lily pond through a cleverly fashioned window, feeling like a minnow or like one of the miniscule snails clinging to the glass. Dark green light and the edges of the lily pad, and above, the Taj Mahal-like flower, serene and opulent.

In the third week of May, at the end of the hiatus of the school year, Charlotte took a walk in the desert gardens at the Huntington. The paradox of the desert being awash with colour enchanted her. She discovered the hothouse, where cuttings and dozens of little pots of blooming cacti, hanging succulents and decades-old plants from Madagascar gave the dry place a fairy-tale quality. She liked the interiority of the space, the outside brought in, the idea of the tree-house reversed. The tree that grew at the end, spilling bright yellow blooms from every branch and splattering the ground with petals, was no taller than Charlotte. She turned corners and greeted a fuzzy fungus-type specimen crowned with a ring of shy fuchsia-like buds already flowering open. Beside it grew low snaky arms ornamented with deep magenta colors. Behind them feathery foliage peeked like lashes on the tips of lethal spikes of thorns. Warm, warm, humid – like a mild sauna – and she felt consoled, understood, by this family of quietly growing, meticulously groomed plants.

She sat down on a bench and pulled out sheets of printed emails from her bag:

Darling –

Here's a something I read on the wall at Norton Simon's newest exhibit:
"I know that great art should be painted with religious feeling. And that was
something I could bring only to the human face. I realised that the artist must
express that within him which is divine. That is why the work of art is a visible
God, and why art is 'a longing for God'." Alexei Jawlensky
I attached one of the pieces from his "faces" series. I thought of you – Colin.

Paris IS transformative, a revelation. I'm sure you must be in love with everything,
chestnut trees and all that walking on the sidewalks. Thank you for realising
Hermes is sexy. Didn't I tell you? I'm sure you fit right in – your "artist" glasses
and your fervent hair – Colin

YES. Will definitely watch Sicko, His work can be polarising, but you can't
be an intelligent, informed member of society without confronting some of these
issues. It's a late night again –yes I am still whistling to an empty lobby at the
wee hours. New York, New York. You make me smile – Colin

Walked in the Huntington gardens today. The desert gardens are my favourite,
so full of life and unexpected – and like you. You straightaway must visit the
Luxembourg and feed the ducks and pretend you are part of the Lost Generation.
You're an absolute Daisy – Colin

Charlotte looked up. Immediately in front of her was a tall slim
saguaro, triple-crowned with fist-sized tufts of flowers. Outside the
hothouse there were three trees with thorns at the base – familiar
trees: they grew at Colin's law school. She had visited him there
when she was still in graduate school and they'd had a fight about
Charlotte looking through the files on his laptop. She couldn't help
herself one afternoon, waiting for Property Law to be over, waiting
and curious and afraid. Since then they had both had moments of

weakness or self-doubt or truly, perhaps, mere and simple loneliness. They had both desired to know the other that was inside, and that daily life so easily screened, when they read each other's emails or journals. But in the last years she had somehow found that fever, the scratching of the itch, slackening until the impulse hardly registered. Until this spring, in one of those late nights of waiting drunk with whisky, lonelier than the dark.

The sick feeling came now in ebbing waves as she observed the fat round barrel cacti, the thin spindly wrists of the fragile-looking tree in the distance. She could not escape the familiarity of some of the phrases of her husband's courtship of another woman. They were partly hers, partly his, like hearing echoes of her life with Colin woven into the fabric of another intimacy. It played like various filters of sound and film in her mind. She remembered his insistence despite her lukewarm response to the suggestion of *Sicko*. She had sent the Jawlensky quote to their pastor in a Christmas letter, and cc'd Colin. He had remarked on it on a ride home, her feet without her shoes on the carpet of the used Jaguar he had just bought.

Paris was their first European city, the low chairs, the fountains, the chestnut trees and the sandy paths and the ache of their walking. She had planned every moment of the six days for months – both of them were new to travel and afraid. She had gone to the Pasadena Public Library and spent hours among the dark basement shelves, studying the glossy pictures in the hardbound copy of *A History of the Gardens of Versailles* (*The gardens of Versailles are perhaps the most famous in the world. The scale of the gardens is monumental, with a sense of openness to the...*), checking out over thirteen books, a cartload of Victor Hugo, Proust, Maupassant, *Monet and His Muse*, language tapes. She had abandoned the attempt at Proust, but read all the catalogues, went through years' worth of *Gourmet* magazines, flipping quickly for any mention of Paris or France. She had consulted the *Guide Michelin* and various maps laid out on their cramped one-bedroom apartment. In the Luxembourg, they had eaten cherries, heavy and pendulous, and doughnut peaches that were roughly the same size. She had wrapped them in a red-checked napkin that she thought seemed French, which she had packed along with the suggested five items every tourist should bring along for the recommended impromptu picnics.

Charlotte stood up inside the hothouse in Pasadena, and carefully, methodically, folded the letters. She creased them, taking her time to make folds, thinking of good origami pleats with thin, flush corners to imitate the beaks of birds, the collar of a shirt, the neck of a swan. She placed them inside the pages of a book she had not planned on bringing – it had lain in her purse for weeks now – and thought of the bookshelf at home where she knew it belonged, the slim gap of space its absence created. She had wondered then where she had put the book, the adjacent neighbouring volumes of poetry now leaning, some slightly askew, their spines loosely held up by their own pages. She knew that when she went home, she would reach up and fit it back into that space and make the line of books upright again, perhaps more tightly so with the addition of these new interleaving papers. She would keep it there, waiting, unobtrusive, unremarkable – but present.

≈℃

My inspiration: This story is inspired by the relationship between Mr Collins and Charlotte Lucas, a pairing that suggests a particularly Austenian villainy and heroism that is neither brazen nor naïve but expressed through the pretensions, betrayals and estrangement of domestic life and the complexities of navigating it as an awakened and sensitive soul.

PEOPLE OF THE BOOK

Holly Dale Bern

People of the Book

❧

Holly Dale Bern

After the retirement of her longtime companion Mrs Jenkinson, and following the felicitous marriages of many close cousins, Anne de Bourgh withdrew most thoroughly from the society of others. What once gave pleasure came to mean nothing or caused pain: cook's meals made Anne bolt from the table; the attempts of visitors to engage or amuse her, she dismissed by turning herself to the wall. No longer did she take the air or drive her pony cart or fashion floral arrangements out of Rosings' abundant, lush blooms. So alarming was Anne's rapid alteration and decline, that Lady Catherine – fearing her only child might not live to inherit dear Rosings – called upon her nephew, Fitzwilliam Darcy, to secure a tutor.

"A woman of thirty-two in need of a tutor?" exclaimed Darcy. "You might better implore me to hire a magician!"

"You *joke* with me, Sir?" cried Lady Catherine, trembling with indignation.

"I mean not to offend, Madam. But a tutor? Good gracious! To what possible end?"

Lady Catherine lurched from her divan. "You have the impudence to *joke?* Anne – ready to be measured for a shroud – and you *scoff?* Be done with it then, and next summoned to engage the undertaker on your cousin's behalf!"

There was no pacifying Lady Catherine. Fearing she would throw an apoplectic fit right then and there, Darcy was left with no choice but to agree to the procurement.

"Pray, what is to be taught?" inquired Elizabeth, at dinner, upon Darcy's return to Pemberley.

"It scarcely matters," said Darcy, with an air of exasperation, "so long as Anne is made lively."

"Can not my cousin Collins oversee this instruction?"

"*Collins?* Come now, Lizzie, you of all people would think that ridiculous."

Elizabeth started to laugh. "I do. I actually do. Can you imagine? Him interrupting before the first page is read, to condole with her. *To condole!*"

Darcy handed Elizabeth her water goblet. "You have turned yourself merry."

"Indeed, I have," said Elizabeth, brushing aside tears of amusement. "I am quite overcome."

"Indeed, you are," said Darcy, displaying no immunity to mirth, himself.

When finally they were composed, and they'd had a few reflective minutes with the mutton, Darcy continued: "What say you to a visit to town? Possibly some among our acquaintance can recommend a tolerant chap."

"Or a tolerable chap!"

"Perhaps we can be so bold as to hope for both."

"Indeed!" said Elizabeth.

Town proved a struggle. Rain fell in chilly sheets, to the accompaniment of battering wind. After several days cooped up at an inn, Darcy and Elizabeth settled their cloaks around their heads and stepped out in a downpour, intent on touring Hans Place no matter the inclemency.

They hadn't walked far when they happened upon a stranger clinging to a fence rail, hallooing up at a tree.

"Shalom, Shalom!" called the man, addressing a small drenched bird huddled high on a limb.

After months of travel, foraging for whatever could sustain life along the road, Benjamin Yaakov, the former brilliant student and follower of Rabbi Simcha Bunim of Peshischa, had dragged himself into London. Benjamin Yaakov was nearly delirious from exhaustion and starvation. And sorrowing for the loss of his faithful mule, Shufflefoot, who – out of gravest necessity – had been bartered for sea passage.

Realising he was being watched, Benjamin Yaakov modified his speech, hailing the bird with "Hallo, Hallo!"

"He surely is mad," whispered Elizabeth.

"Hallo, yourself!" said Darcy, stepping toward the stranger.

The young man recoiled. And well he should; he was coated cap to boot in filth. But then he spoke: "I am Benjamin Yaakov, this very day from Poland. I hoped I might persuade yonder finch to make a gift of a cherry, for I am famished."

"Poland?" said Darcy, astonished. "Do I hear right? *Poland?"*

"The very same," replied Benjamin Yaakov. He was about to say more, but Darcy held up his hand.

"Save your speech, man," said he. "It will not do for a traveler to remain starving in a torrent."

With that, Benjamin Yaakov was led to the inn and treated to a hot meal of biscuits and stew. Between bowls, and while they waited for the innkeeper to prepare a bath and fetch clean clothes, Benjamin Yaakov, in English slightly but charmingly accented, told of his long, wretched journey and of the grievous loss of Shufflefoot. He disclosed that he possessed a proficiency with language, a knowledge of the various religions and geographies of the world, an adeptness with song and dance, and that he was seeking employment and lodging.

He did not tell the Darcys that the languages within his mastery numbered nine. Nor did he reveal that the pursuit of his family's goat, strayed deep into the forest, had saved him from the murdering pillagers who had burned down his shtetl. Most assuredly, he did not let them know that he was a Jew.

When the innkeeper returned with fresh clothing, Darcy suggested that the guest's worn garments be sent to the rubbish.

"Ah no!" cried Benjamin Yaakov, dropping his spoon. "I must keep some of this."

Hurriedly, he gathered from beneath his tattered cloak a silk shawl and a pair of black kidskin boxes. The boxes were of a size to hold a baby's coral beads and tethered to long leather straps.

"What goes in them?" Elizabeth asked, as Benjamin Yaakov hastily folded the foreign-looking apparatus into the shawl and, with no small amount of blushing, slid the newly made bundle behind his back.

"Spices," replied Benjamin Yaakov, quickly adding that none remained.

Having vowed to hide his religion evermore, he was unwilling to admit that within those boxes, on special kosher parchment, were the many Hebrew names of God, along with His reminder to live righteously – and that he, Benjamin Yaakov, faithfully wore those phylacteries on his forehead and left arm each weekday morning, as commanded by Exodus and Deuteronomy.

"The man is a mystic," Darcy whispered to Elizabeth.

Elizabeth said it must be so, for she had never before beheld such a creature. "We need mind his exhaustion," she told Darcy.

Which they did. Waiting three full days while Benjamin Yaakov dove into slumber in a quiet room secured for his restoration.

When finally he awoke, the Darcys were pleased to find him an amiable fellow of no little refinement, approximate to them in age, and more than passably pleasant in appearance.

"A bird-charmer, a scholar, a mystic," said Elizabeth, out of Benjamin Yaakov's hearing.

"Un-housed into the bargain," said Darcy. "What say you we turn him toward Rosings?"

"I say – most assuredly it must be tried."

After the arrival of Benjamin Yaakov, Anne – forced to the parlor by her mother – stubbornly attached her gaze to the wallpaper and spoke not a word. Benjamin Yaakov remained several days in her presence – silently, patiently – with only the clock's chirping cuckoo to bid him well. Finally, when it seemed Anne would not be unfrozen, Benjamin Yaakov embarked on her healing, folding his hands in a benediction and chanting the *Mi Sheberach* over her head.

He had not even arrived at *habrakha l'imoteinu* when Anne de Bourgh spun around.

"You curse me!" she shrieked, rising to flee.

"I bless you, Dear Lady," said Benjamin Yaakov, appalled to be accused of anything but good will. He caught her by the arm to prevent her from leaving.

And then he caught her eye.

"What call you that strange tongue?" murmured Anne, crumbling onto the couch.

"It goes by 'Hebrew,'" replied Benjamin Yaakov.

"Bless me again," whispered Anne. "Oh! Bless me and bless me."

*

What followed from there were hours of unburdening. Benjamin – making Anne the exception to his secrecy rule – explained all that it was to be a Jew, and how he had loved his years in Peshischa before the pogram. Anne told of a life so strictly conscribed, so dictated by regard for wealth and rank, so utterly underpinned by disdain for others, that, oftentimes, she hardly knew if she could, or even wanted to, draw her next breath.

Lady Catherine, of course, apprehended none of this. And weeks later, delighted that tutoring had produced such an excellent improvement in her daughter, she declared Benjamin Yaakov a prince from the continent. A prince come to hide away at Rosings after rebellion had robbed him of his throne. Consequently, she accorded him the respect and attention she believed such an elevated station demanded. At the same time, observing a growing devotion between the pair, she urged them to wed.

It took a while, but finally Benjamin broached the subject. They were under a rose bower on a gentle summer day, when he, reading to Anne from the Book of Ruth, paused after reciting "thy people shall be my people, and your God, my God."

"Pray, do not stop," said Anne.

Benjamin sighed. Stood, paced, heavily sighed some more – until with unsteady voice, he spoke, the book held close to his chest: "As well you know, you have grown dear to me, Anne. But I have only poverty to bestow. And these words from Ruth. So I entreat you – let it be thus between us. Let me leap to your faith. Let me adorn myself in the Christ of your family.

"Marry me!"

"That shall not do!" cried Anne. *"That* I could not bear!"

Benjamin had not intended to weep. Now though, believing himself severely denied, he could not prevent himself from sobbing. "You do not love me," he lamented, unable to face her.

"Indeed!" spoke Anne, taking her handkerchief to his eyes. "I love you so very well, that *your* people shall be *my* people!"

"Impossible!" said Benjamin, turning to her in disbelief. "It lies beyond contemplation."

"Ah! But I insist upon it. I utterly insist!"

"*You* would be a Jew? – the most despised of earth?"

"I would take up a mantle of prejudice, yes! – and with gladness!" Anne replied boldly, "if I might be yours and you mine."

For minutes after that, there was nothing but tears on both sides, and much gazing and longing.

"We must never say 'Jewish,' never speak of it," Benjamin cautioned when they were again ready for words, "unless it be to each other or to another Jew. It is a fault in me – I declare it – but I am too proud to enlist for the hatred of others."

"Be at peace," said Anne. "I will follow you in observing secrecy for the rest of my days."

After Mr Collins married them, Lady Catherine, out of consideration for propriety, moved to an elegant cottage within the estate and assigned the daily running of Rosings to Anne and her prince. Without ado, the hogs were sold and replaced with cattle and sheep. The kitchen was made kosher; though without a rabbi's blessing, it was not as utterly kosher as a devout Jewish couple would wish it. Still – a start. From town, Anne ordered four sets of china and four sets of silver, sufficient to divide meat and dairy for every day and meat and dairy for Passover. Anne mustered the cook to recreate the meals of Benjamin's childhood: kugel and tsimmes and cholent. A braided egg bread, the challah, became part of the weekend meals. With tender grace, and oftentimes grateful tears, Anne blessed the Shabbos candles and joined her husband in sipping Sabbath wine.

Together, Anne and Benjamin explored Rosings' ample library.

Had it been there all along? Understood only as a place for dining and gossip and cards? Benjamin showed Anne which books deserved her attention, helped her develop a love of ideas and learning. Under starry night skies, he taught her to dance, taught her to sing – as he, himself, had been taught by the joyous disciples of The Baal-Shem Tov.

One afternoon, Anne led a beautiful young mule, decked in a daisy wreath, into the yard. "My wedding gift to you," she told her husband. "I hope you will teach him to come for carrots in at least nine languages."

Benjamin was so overwhelmed, he could not speak. By the way he held her, he did not need to.

At Anne's urging, Benjamin wrote to the Jews of Peshischa: *If any of you survive, come to us. You will find a home here.* He enclosed a map.

To their vast delight – though two years passed before they knew of it – the invitation journeyed into proper hands. Benjamin was outdoors one morning, communing with Shufflefoot II, when – like sight returned to the blind – a rabbi appeared. None other than Itzkar Yaakov, Benjamin's younger brother!

If it may be said that among dancers there are those who kick their heels to heaven, then it happened on that day; there was that kind of dancing. There was that kind of singing. After a sufficiency of time for hugging and crying and leaping to touch the cheek of God – many days of that sort of celebration – the kitchen received a rabbinic koshering, and a truly kosher bridal cake was prepared.

One perfect Sunday while Lady Catherine lay napping in her cottage, blissfully convinced that her daughter had married royalty – and with only themselves and the birds of the sky as witnesses, and Rabbi Itzkar Yaakov presiding – Anne and Benjamin wed again as a Jewish bride and groom.

True to the promises made on the day of their betrothal, they never spoke of their Judaism, except to each other or within the close-lipped privacy of their Jewish orbit.

But yet – there is a thing with the wind. It carries secrets. However well guarded, however unspoken. And a secret once known may well be a secret in need of response. One day, not long after the Jewish wedding, and a year before the birth of their son, Lewis Yaakov, a gift in elaborate wrapping arrived from Pemberley. A book. A bible. Bound in royal blue velvet, with magnificent color illustrations. The Old Testament. And a card: *May joy reside in your hearts, now and always. Yours with abiding affection, Elizabeth and Fitzwilliam Darcy.*

As joy was wished, so it was received. For the five decades of the Yaakov's married life, likely no more adoring couple ever graced Kent, and great good flowed from their union. Polish Jews were saved. A Jewish community took root. After a while there were enough Jewish men for a minyon, and Benjamin Yaakov was finally able to chant the prayer of remembrance for his family and for the lost Jews of Peshischa.

In the area around what was once Rosings Park, a small, hidden-away shul still stands. Occasionally, visitors arrive to visit there and pray. There are ancient torah scrolls, intricate woodwork to admire. Meticulous needlepoint hangings, a nearly two-hundred-year-old eternal flame. Under glass – a much cherished Old Testament on display. This bible served, and serves still, as a record keeper for a Jewish family started long ago: parents, two sons and two daughters, grandchildren, great-grandchildren, on and on. With one line – neatly penned, unsigned – on the inverse side of the faded velvet cover:

Bless me again. Oh! bless me and bless me.

My inspiration: Believing that heroism resides in deeds of subtle delicacy as well as grander gestures, I wished to give Elizabeth and Fitzwilliam Darcy, and the de Bourgh ladies too, a different kettle of prejudice with which to contend. What would they make of a brilliant and appealing, though penniless, foreigner – a true scapegoat on the world stage? I hoped that an admixture of mercy, abundant kindness and a willingness to tread beyond the expected – along with a dose of Lady Catherine's misapprehension – would produce something satisfying.

THE DARCY SYNDROME

Les Wood

The Darcy Syndrome

✣

Les Wood

OK

So we're going to start again then (again), from the top.

One for Memory Lane.

It's been a while since we've been down here… we must be in need of some major internal emotional propping up.

And for this episode, I will be wearing the lad from the cheese counter at Sainsbury's who is hot but clearly out of the question on account of age, which categorically improves his appeal…

In fact – if we're really honest about it it's possible he's not much older than your son.

But what the hell. I don't quibble. That's not my job.

Just a sec while I clear my throat, check my teeth for unsightly broccoli bits and straighten my white cheese-counter jacket and face piercings…

Oh. No jacket then.

Well obviously I'd agree; how could anyone be expected to excel romantically in a festering grubby work overall, in the firm knowledge that there are curd particles decomposing within inches of ones finest performance? Sacrilege.

Unless of course – that turns you on..?

I have to be honest though… the face piercings are causing me some difficulty… You like them? Fine. Whatever you say – they stay. And the tattoos?

Okay.

So it's outdoors, contemporary twenty-first century and with designer-style-type-smart-but-cool jacket and trousers (because this specific individual would look a complete fanny in a cravat) of no particular description cos they just ain't important enough to warrant one.

With the piercings.

Apparel of course, really has only a very minor role. Much as it's important to get it right – and it's important to get everything absolutely spot on to the point of being obsessional – and very occasionally will become an issue for a brief, passing thought (such as the wet shirt… Oh… the wet shirt…); physicality is merely peripheral here in my world. "Getting it right" translates as "getting it so comfortable you don't notice it…" There are higher concerns at stake here.

And *not* with the previously hot and popular bald chap with the bloody gorgeous brown eyes and epic long eyelashes from the garage who smiles nicely and usually flirts disgracefully with you every time you go in cos he over-charged you today and didn't serve you personally but let the spotty malodorous little oik with paint stripper breath and boils of Satan do his dirty work for him and tell you about having to replace the splange sprockets or something which hiked the price up an extra 47 fucking quid…which means no babysitter this weekend which will not now be spent out with the girls but in with a book and—

Me.

So he's well out of favour and not worthy of a second thought. Let alone inclusion in your personal therapy. Nope. Just the jailbait from the deli counter who vaguely caught your interest. With the one gloomy eye unobscured by the emo fringe. You're not really there for this one are you…? I know – I know! It's not my business.

Ah but never mind; give it a go. You never know. Might have potential. They all have potential. We can always tweak him about a bit…

Ready? 3…2…1…

"You still have me pegged as an arrogant stuck-up snob then?" I ask quietly, and even *I'm* having a little difficulty here. Grunge-boy and snob? It's about as incongruous as a beetle and a blowjob.

I'm compliantly looking down in submission as I speak but slowly raise my yearning gaze to her face to gauge the response as I finish the question. I'm standing close but not touching (not yet… we have to build up to that gradually) and (well, I *was* created by a woman to be fair) demurely and rather effeminately brush my hair away from my Cyclops eye so I can look really smitten at her. The fringe is definitely getting in the way.

I make an effort to look desperate, pleading, pitiful, even pathetic. Order of the day. Need and want. The more desperation, the better… But sexy too.

Oh ye gods, I'm good!

Actually, when it boils down to it, this part is a one-man performance, since there's very rarely any input from the recipient at this juncture. There's no necessity. It's my behaviour which is of vital import; she instinctively knows what her response is and will always be, without any need for words; just raw, unchecked, unfettered, gut-wrenching emotion which she can deal with entirely on her own. She doesn't plan to argue exactly.

For an infinite, wonderful moment in time – and as often as she likes – she can be entirely perfect and experience the Engulfing Orgasmic Ecstasy of being desired by the most beautiful, captivating, sexy, alluring significant other she can imagine, create or perceive; and no one, but *no* one can interfere, laugh, belittle or take it away. It's hers. Total control. Absolute power. Consummate, pure, sublime felicity. Bugger Romance – positive raw emotional gratification. Free.

I give her that. I am the catalyst and the vessel. I am the therapy, self-induced, self inflicted, self-choreographed. I am truly acquiescent and can be moulded to whatever shape or personality as and when required and I can be as good, bad or indifferent as my hostess can fancy... And so, so safe!

I am the epitome of flawlessness. An infinite improvement on the real thing eh?

Even as Cheese-boy.

But enough bragging. Back to work.

My next function is the facial configuration of absolute bliss followed by the sexiest kiss she can either recall, or failing that, envisage.
Usually, of course, we do a few repeats here; slight alterations to wording, venue, angle of snog etc. Mostly dependent on time; not so many repeats if we happen to be briefly kicking heels in a supermarket queue or a traffic jam – but if we're walking the dog or on a long tedious bus journey, repetition can get a bit monotonous and in the end we both get bored. Sometimes I even find myself wishing we could take a break and do something sort-of "normal", like nip down the pub for a game of pool or have a damn good shag or something while I can sense her checking her nails or compiling her shopping list or mentally searching for the earring she couldn't find this morning.

But this is not going so well and I'm not entirely surprised. Couple of tries and I've sincerely given it my best despite the ridiculous and obscene metalwork in my lips... but I can tell her heart's not really in it.

In fact...

She's... faking!

Maybe it's the tongue piercing... or the fringe. I doubt his being barely out of trainer pants is helping either if we're really frank about it.

Naturally, its nothing whatsoever to do with me because of course, as usual, *I* am performing at peak no matter what materials I'm given to work with. I have no significance in that respect. I am a facilitator. Nothing more. No responsibility. No real input. I am created to your requirements, I fulfil your desires to the best of my ability and bugger off with no credits (uh... yeah...) at the end.

Best bet is to have a break and a think about a more suitable candidate. There's always Colin and his wet shirt if all else fails...

Actually, I quite enjoy doing Colin and his wet shirt. It's the standard starter for most of my clients, as is the script, and it comes so naturally now, it flows freely. I don't even have to think about what to say anymore if I don't care to. Occasionally I ad-lib if I get a bit bored or inspired, but usually I get hauled back into line fairly sharpish and I don't seem to mind.

There's not so much demand for the original package nowadays though. Gets less and less by the year. Mostly we've "been there, done that" to death within months, days or even hours of contracting the Darcy Syndrome (in the case of some of my more experienced or advanced clientele!). But it will always be my favourite stage; the newness, the excitement, the energy.... My ladies are at their most receptive and most easily satisfied in this phase, so my work is that much more personally fulfilling, and I have that minor element of "control" over events for its short duration which makes it all the more appealing. Nowadays, these encounters are more likely to be fewer and farther in between – simply due to the fact that most fresh initiates are youngish students introduced via the education system. They start off by studying me for exams and then discover that I'm an imaginable source of inspiration in so many more ways...

And there's the foreign contingent... Now that I'm translated into every conceivable language, I find I'm being adopted and adapted by cultures I can't even begin to comprehend! Chinese, Russian, Venezuelan... the list goes on and on as does my repertoire and ability to adjust. I love it! I have to admit to a slight endearment to those more obscure nationalities who have me perform my magic in language, attire and bizarre venues that would so captivate The Author! I've given my all in goat herders' huts, up the Eiffel Tower, by volcanoes, in traditional humble farm lanes, extravagant hotel balconies... you name it.

I've helped the short, fat, tall, slender, elegant, ugly, fascinating, plastic, sad, angry, depressed, interesting, dull, immense, insignificant, rich, poor, bereft and accomplished alike. Gratitude is gratitude whatever hue it takes.

I'm so modest...

But work.

Hang on...

I can't interest you in a wicked wet shirt moment then? Not even wearing the delectable and delicious Colin – master of the dewy-eye Darcy phenomenon?

This is serious…

Uh-ohh… I'm not feeling the love here… this is one of those rarer sensations which momentarily permeate from time to time when there's a concentration lapse and the outside shit leaches in… Don't like them much myself and they aren't generally welcome since "here" is actually supposed to be a haven *away* from all that crap…

What they do is push me out.

You're… am I getting this right – pissed off with me?

Hold up here… you conceived me. You called me into existence to fill a gaping hole in your emotional internal fabric; ripped open by external malevolent influences way, way, way beyond your control… You choose who I represent and where and how. I'm nothing short of your very own unique fictitious version of a nineteenth-century literary creation originally devised to poke a perverse comedic jibe at ridiculous, inflexible and restrictive contemporary societal rules. I have no place in the twenty-first century other than my inadvertent romantic adoption as a sex object, thanks to Colin and his wet shirt. I doubt The Author intended me as an emotional therapist for far more women than I can count – but I just do the job anyway. And usually with good grace. But you're not supposed to get pissed off with me…

Okay. I geddit.

It's because what I actually do is make every man you meet look defective, because I'm a totally unrealistic benchmark even though I'm not real and have no substance.

And today Reality is Striking Home.
Through Cheese-boy?

It's not Cheese-boy then. It's fantasy that is the problem.

It's not enough…? Something is missing?

You have more imagination than Cheese-boy….

There's a crisis going on here… time for a break I'm feeling.

I shall quietly back away into a dark and empty recess, where I can take off Brie-boy and the cheese jacket. And wait.

Sorry – what was that?

She moved quickly down the crowded street, dodging her way between the myriads of dark and faceless people all scurrying about their individual business. No two alike and yet every one of them exactly the same. So many of them… different directions, different lives, different looks, personalities, needs, objectives. And yet, all of one species. One type. With common basic purpose. Mating, procreation, followed ultimately by death. With a whole bunch of complicated shite chucked in to make it just that tad less tedious.

Fuck. What a cynic I'm getting to be, she thought.

She charged on, knocking into people now – pushing them out of her path. After all, why should she move out of their way? She was just as important in the general scheme of things as any of these flabby, ugly buggers. For all she knew, she could be the only REAL person in existence; all these others could just be figments of her hilarious imagination... wasn't there a philosophy based around that? Existentialism or something? Nah... that was the one about taking responsibility in a hostile universe or some such nonsense. She'd look it up when she got home. There's so many damn philosophical "isms" to get confused by... Why does everything have to be so bloody complicated? Even thinking had to get heavy and hard work now. Sometimes she wished she'd been born thick. If she only had just a handful of brain cells to bounce around inside her calcific skull, then she wouldn't be troubled by these damn pretentious meditations which plagued her night and day and confused her so righteously.

"Do you ever wish you were totally, mind-numbingly, stark staring dense?" she asked Fitz – her current bed partner and one she had plans to keep for a while cos he had a cute arse, nice teeth, cleaned the sink and toilet occasionally and agreed with her most of the time on the basis that it made life more bearable...

Um... I like the bit about the cute arse...

We're not wet-shirting then?

Are we creating instead?

Are we writing?

Have we actually moved on to a new phase which not many of my clients achieve but which is my absolute ultimate goal because that's what I sincerely believe MY hero – The Author – would wish for...? For an enthusiastic writer to have been inspired by one of her heroes always gave her such pleasure!

I'm sure she would laugh heartily to see her adored Darcy venerated and worshipped even as I currently am, but I have no hesitation in believing that she would rather her legacy be that of promoting the written word than of a therapeutic sex object. To witness one of my lovely ladies grow from emotional fuckwit to aspiring author is an honour and a rare privilege for which I am eternally grateful to The Author!

I'm happy to report that my client is no longer my client – she's too busy typing. (It's a bit of an improvement on quills and pencils – and blotchy old ink!)

Best get on; guess I should be looking for a new job then…

You wouldn't happen to know of any young ladies who have yet to be introduced to the illustrious works of Miss Jane Austen, by any chance…?

❧

My inspiration: Romantic heroes are always utilised by the woman of discernment as an object of fantasy – there can be no denying that and I guess I am no different. I liked the idea of hearing from the haughty Darcy now reduced to sex object… from *his* angle. Having gotten used to his new role, I feel he would surely still retain his superior conceit and I actually thoroughly enjoyed working with him in this piece!

It matters not how Jane Austen effects her inspiration to write; through literary or fantasy routes, but to my mind that would be her ultimate legacy.

POSKE

Jocelyn Watson

Poske

Jocelyn Watson

Auntie reminds me all the time I must thank God, and I do. Every night before khana, we all kneel around the altar of Our Lady the Virgin Mary. Every day Auntie puts fresh white frangipani on the altar, and if she can't get frangipani, she puts white mogra or jasmine and a wonderful scent fills the room. Uncle coughs and everyone is quiet. Then he begins the rosary, then Nana and then Dada, then Auntie, then Lorso, then Joki, then Lazar, then Nikel, then Mingel, then Pedru, then me, then our mestha, who has cooked for the family since before Lorso was born, then Rosanna who looks after Nana, then Minnie Mai who has looked after all of us since we were small, and finally their blessing from God, Antoinette, who always says the final Hail Mary. Everyday I thank him because of what he has done for me; but now, now he must not welcome my thanks.

In the narrow lanes of Girgaum, away from the dust and the dirt, away from the cars, the motorcycles and the taxis blowing their damn horns, away from the sleeping cows, away from the poor waking and cleaning themselves in the street, away from the cries of the chai wallahs, the dabba wallahs, and the attar wallahs, is Khotachiwadi. They say, for I don't know, that Khotachiwadi is like a village in Goa. But what is correct is that there is no place like

Khotachiwadi in all of Bombay. I know because I have been to many places in Bombay.

When Nettie and I were small, we were only supposed to play in the lanes of Khotachiwadi, but we followed the boys. Where they went, we went. We walked over the pebbly beach, onto the fishing boats anchored at Cuff Parade, to Apollo Bunder, to the Gateway to watch the boats sail off for Elephanta. We went to Flora Fountain and, when Lorso or Lazar had a few rupees to spare, they would let us share a pony ride at Bandstand. We followed the boys as they marched down Colaba Causeway looking at the shops, the bhel poori stands, the hawkers and the street stalls. Nettie and I loved the fabric shops with their cottons and their saris. Best of all we loved the glass bangle stalls. We would try them on: blue ones, green ones, orange ones, red ones, silver and gold. We would mix them till our arms were like rainbows and the banglewallahs, fed up with us not buying, would shoo us away. We marched behind the boys and when it became late, we ran behind as they shouted, "jaldi karo, jaldi karo!" Pedru would look back and wink and we would smile.

Sometimes on Sunday we would go to Regal or Strand, for we loved films but often there wasn't enough money. We would go with the boys to their friends' home and climb the stairs to the top of the building and watch. The blue sky came like a patterned sari, with kites of green or yellow or pink, flying higher and higher to heaven. The boys used maanja and we watched, excited, as the glass-coated string cut through another's and his kite sank, defeated, to the ground.

On other days we had to be home by seven. One time Lazar missed the rosary. He tried to creep upstairs unseen but Uncle was sitting there, waiting, his face like an angry Shiva. We all watched from the top of the stairs as Uncle took Lazar's head and banged it hard against the wall. Uncle knew that he had been playing cricket in the Maidan because someone had told him. In Khotachiwadi everybody knows what you do.

The houses here are only small, with one storey, and made of wood. Some are painted green or yellow or blue with long verandahs across the front where everyone sits. Each has a back courtyard and there is a staircase outside to get to the top bedroom where all the boys sleep. The family room is upstairs. On the wall are pictures of our Lord, and the Virgin Mary, and a black and white photograph of Uncle and Auntie's wedding.

We know everyone in Khotachiwadi – the Garcias, the Baptistas, the Ferreiras, the D'Souzas, the Fernandez – everyone. We call to them from our bedroom windows, from the verandahs; we can smell if they are having vindaloo or xacuti or Bombay duck and sometimes we too can hear if there is a fight. We are in and out of each other's houses, and when we were children we walked together to St Teresa's Convent. Elizabeth Rowe was the Headmistress when Nettie and I were there. I remember once she told me to be proud of myself, and I thought, "Why you are saying this to me?" but now I think back to those words.

We are friendly with the Sharmas and Mehtas and the other Hindu families, but it is mainly the East Indians, the Goans and the Catholics that we spend time with. At Christmas there is always a party, everyone comes, even Father Remedios. He knows each member of his flock and their troubles, but not mine. For the marriages and the feast days we decorate Khotachiwadi with paper lanterns and make cribs and string coloured paper from one home to another. The lanes of Khotachiwadi fill with music. Nikel and Mingel play guitar and the Ferreira family are all good singers. They sing Konkani songs and Portuguese songs and movie songs and we dance. Nettie and I love to dance. We dance with each other whenever we can at the Pound Parties, at Christmas and on Feast Days, and the boys laugh at us but we don't care.

I have lived all my eighteen years here with the Brittos. They have treated me like one of their family but I am not. I am poske. They say I was born in Morjim, in Goa. I have never seen my mother. She left me with the Carmelite nuns and ran away. All Auntie's babies were boys and after Pedru she stopped dreaming of having a girl. She thought God wanted her only to have sons. The Jesus and Mary sisters told her about me and so I became their poske. They treated me like their daughter, not like a poske, and then a year later Nettie came. I can hear Auntie's prayers of joy and thanks that at last she had a baby girl.

The boys are good to us. They tease us but teach us also, so I'm a fast bowler and Nettie's hitting is good. Mostly Auntie and Uncle treat me the same, same new clothes, same food, same schools. But Nettie has piano lessons. Her teacher is always saying she doesn't practise enough. I try to push her but she's stubborn and won't listen. Auntie and Uncle want her to be a teacher but she doesn't want. I'm thinking to be a teacher is a good thing, but Auntie and Uncle think I have a better chance for a job looking after little ones. Nettie doesn't think this will suit me, and I don't think so too, but what to do?

The room that Nettie and I share is a small room. The walls are covered with paintings that she and I have done. We draw each other and can see from our paintings and photos how much we have changed. Nettie's eyes are still the same, big and strong, and when she smiles it is like she is telling you to open your heart to her. My eyes need glasses. Sometimes people ask if we are sisters because together, in our uniforms or our dresses, we look the same: same S size, same 36 shoes, same 24 inch waist and same long, black hair that shines because we always put on Furtado's Best Coconut Oil.

Nettie and I found out about the "monthly business" together. No one told us. Nana said nothing. Auntie said nothing. We thought we had some serious illness and didn't know what to do or who to ask. We told Minnie Mai, and she gave us some rags, which she said we must use and wash each month and that we were big girls now. Slowly we learnt so much together. When one felt sad, both felt sad. Whenever we were worried about school or anything we talked to each other. The other day Nettie said, "We should just run away."

We laughed.

"Where should we go?" I asked.

"To Calcutta. To Goa."

"I want to stay here in Khotachiwadi."

"But as long as we are here we…"

Nettie didn't finish the sentence and while I was sitting on the bed waiting, Joki called us to prayers. Lorso is already twenty-six and Joki twenty-five, so last month the family prayers were for them and their futures. They will marry soon, two girls from Khotachiwadi, Frances and Ena. When we were little girls Francis and Ena played with us running up and down the lanes. We liked to watch the kallaiwallah who comes every week. We would all run outside when we heard him call banging his pots and pans. All the Aunties in Khotachiwadi would give him their pots. He would pour only a little drop from his bottle, and scrub and polish so that even the darkest, dirtiest handi would shine like silver and we would all think the kallaiwallah was a magician from the circus.

The Christmas season will soon be over and we must decide what we will do. When we talk to the other girls in Khotachiwadi they are thinking about their marriages, but that is not what Nettie and I want. We want something different.

"Mari, I want to be with you."

"Nettie, what nonsense you talking now? You are with me."

I am not as brave as Nettie. But she is not poske. I know that Uncle and Auntie can ask me to leave.

Last month all were excited for Nettie because she was accepted at St Xavier's. What to say? My mind is all mixed up. I walked along Chowpatty Beach. When I returned to Khotachiwadi there were a lot of people in the house. Aunties and Uncles had come to congratulate Auntie and Uncle. Though many of the Hindu families don't send their girls to college, Auntie and Uncle want Nettie to have a good education and become a teacher. Auntie explained to me that it costs a lot of money to go to college. She said again I could get a good job looking after chota bacca. I said nothing.

Last week the Lobos left Khotachiwadi. Auntie said the boy, David, who is the same age as Nikel, brought terrible shame on the family. When Nettie and I asked what happened, Auntie didn't say. That night we talked in bed.

"Did you know the Lobos have left?"

"I knew nothing. I was so shocked."

"I like David, always laughing. He didn't have a girlfriend. I asked Nikel and even he didn't know."

"So strange."

"We don't even know where they have gone to."

"Far away."

"I wish I knew why."

"Better not to know."

"Mari, perhaps we should go far away."

"What, starting that nonsense again, and here you are at Xavier's and you want to run away."

"I don't understand."

"I too don't understand."

"Mari, I know with you by my side I feel strong."

"Nettie I too…"

"You what?"

"I too know that you and Khotachiwadi are here within me."

When Nettie went to St Xavier's, I thought I would lose her forever. She came home three months ago and told me that she had read about scholarships to study abroad. She brought home papers. After khana we went to our room saying that Nettie had to study. We filled in the papers and waited. We didn't tell anyone. When we knelt for the rosary Nettie and I had our own prayers. Then one day before the monsoon arrived, Auntie was surprised when the postman came with two letters, one for Nettie and one for me.

"What is this?" Auntie asked.

"We must open to find out, no?" Nettie answered.

We wanted to run to our room. But Auntie told us to open the letters in front of her. Nettie's letter told her that she had been successful. Auntie was shocked. Nettie looked at me. "Jaldi karo. Jaldi karo," she shouted.

Nettie took my letter from me and tore it open.

"Mari, Mari," she screamed throwing her arms around me.

For one month Uncle and Auntie would not agree. Nana and Dada would not agree. Father Remedios did not think it was safe for two young girls to go alone to England.

Only Nikel, Mingel and Pedru said let us go. There was a big tamasha. Nettie and I went to see Ms Elizabeth Rowe and she came to speak to Uncle and Auntie, telling them that the world was changing and an education was a valuable thing, and to get a scholarship was a great gift and for the family to get two was a blessing from God that we must not refuse.

❧

My inspiration: I was inspired by *Persuasion*, which I read as a novel of second chances, expectations of one's society and the constancy of love. I would like to think that my short story is a multicultural, twenty-first century adaptation of the role of the family, of the pressures women encounter in seeking fulfilment, encased in a simple love story.

JW'S REDEMPTION

Elaine Grotefeld

JW's Redemption

sc

Elaine Grotefeld

Before the bathroom mirror, Jason Warner flexed his biceps, tensed his six-pack abs. What to wear tonight – the lilac shirt, or plain white? He lathered his chiselled face with L'Occitaine Cade shaving foam, lifted his razor and gashed himself across the chin. *What the hell?* He leant over the sink for a minute, watched blood drip on to white porcelain. What was with him today? First, there'd been the incident over in West Vancouver. He was about to close on a magnificent cliff-top property; this family from Hong Kong were so keen they didn't care how much it cost – so Jason had smoothly raised the owner's asking price by a few hundred grand. Immediately, he felt himself being shoved to the edge of the deck – as if by invisible hands – where he had to grab the railings and squat to avoid plunging into the grey sea below. The family conferred at length in Cantonese – and shook their heads. "Haunted," the son explained.

Jason tore a tissue into strips and dabbed the wound. Thank God the dog bite hadn't cut through flesh this afternoon. That was the second incident: he'd called on old Mrs Schmidt, charmed her sufficiently to let him list her water-front property – even got her to agree to a commission rate above the norm. When she was about to sign, he'd tripped over her elderly Alsatian – didn't even see it – who

179

promptly bit him in the leg. Mrs Schmidt took this as a sign – and tore up the contract.

And now he'd lacerated his face. He kept dabbing the blood, and then applied neat tea-tree oil. It stung like hell. The phone rang in the living room, and he let the machine pick up.

"Hi, Jason – it's Liz. I'm calling to find out what time you'd like me to come over tonight. I've got everything organised and am all set to prove to you that English food is a lot more than fish and chips. Call me at home. Bye."

Damn – he'd forgotten. He'd met Liz about six months ago, soon after she moved to Vancouver from London. He liked the way she spoke, her intelligence, her sense of humour, her *naturalness*. He'd expected to sleep with her after the first or second date – but it still hadn't happened. Her reserve alternately vexed and intrigued him. Fortunately he had other friends who were more open in that department.

Jason continued to shave – with extreme care – while considering his options.

Option One: he could cancel his dinner date with Mrs Diane Davenport, the spectacularly wealthy and famous New York fashion designer, who was in Vancouver for a photo shoot and who'd invited Jason out to dinner. They'd met at a drinks party where she'd picked him out like a pair of Jimmy Choos. She was still beautiful too – albeit in that clenched, defiant way that super-fit 40- or even 50-something women can be. She had homes in New York, London, Paris and a 60-foot yacht in the Caribbean. So... forget Option One.

Option Two: call Liz back, fabricate an excuse. But she was no fool, she'd see through him – and it would be so *awkward*.

Actually, there was only one option – ignore the message.

Diane Davenport was already seated at the table when Jason strolled in to the *Market* restaurant, first floor of the new Four Seasons downtown. Mahogany-coloured bamboo lined the walls; tea-lights cast a low, flickering glow across the dark-wood tables.

"Nervous getting ready, were we?" she said, eyeing the plaster he'd forgotten (damn!) to remove from his chin... and gestured for him to sit not opposite, but next to her. Her voice was low and gravelly. She wore a low-cut white shirt which, even in this low light, showed the fine lines on her chest. But the golf-ball emerald at her throat set off her green eyes beautifully.

While they talked, Jason savoured the ambiguity of her ankle grazing against his. She told him she was thinking of buying a property in Vancouver – around the $10 million mark. Perhaps he could show her some places. He forgot about the plaster. Her extreme wealth intoxicated him – the heady Chanel perfume; the diamond-encrusted watch on her thin, tanned wrist; the expensively ironed face. Jason tried to dress the part – but as with most things, on credit. The harbour-view, 12th floor apartment was his – at least for the six months a year that his parents took off, determined to spend their entire retirement savings on high-end world cruises. For the rest of the year he rented elsewhere.

"My place or yours?" Mrs Davenport said, after pointedly claiming the bill as hers.

Later, Jason opened the door and led Mrs Davenport in, relieved he'd paid the cleaning lady to do extra time today. An immaculate pad in Coal Harbour, gazing north across the water to Stanley Park and the white-flecked, oddly two dimensional North Shore mountains behind – nothing to be ashamed of.

The place was a wreck. CDs and books were scattered on and under the glass coffee table; empty beer cans and dirty boxer shorts littered the wooden floor. The air whiffed of pig manure.

"I – I don't know what's happened here," Jason said, trying not to sound shrill. *Who had a key?* He never gave any of them a key. "It wasn't like this when I left."

"You didn't mention you had a room-mate," Mrs Davenport said, coolly.

"Only a temporary one." From the kitchen, came a man's voice – with a clipped, English accent.

"Who's there?" Jason said.

Seconds later, a strange-looking man appeared before them in the living room. Medium build, medium height and extremely clean shaven. He was dressed like an actor in some period drama – scarlet waistcoat with silver buttons, white cravat, knee-length pants and white stockings, rather grubby at the bottom. The buttons were starting to pull a little tight on the waistcoat. Early 30s – about Jason's age – with a mop of brown hair and a touch of the familiar about his even-featured face.

Jason was conscious of Diane by his side, watching him.

The man gave a theatrical wave of his arm –and bowed. "Good Evening, Mr Warner," he said.

"Who the hell are *you*, and why are you here?"

"*Why am I here?* You invited me, remember?" Mrs Davenport said, an edge to her tone. "I was promised champagne – and a spectacular view."

Jason turned to her – and back to the stranger. "I'm sorry," he said, "I have no idea who this man is."

She tried her best to frown, scanned the room. "What man?"

The man started whistling, looking about the room, tapping his dirty shoe. Now Jason wanted to punch him. "The lady must leave."

"Will you shut up!"

"I beg your pardon." Mrs Davenport spoke as if through clenched teeth.

"No, I didn't mean you, I was talking to him... that man there... can you not see him?"

"I see nobody but you." She backed away. "You know what?" she said, heading for the door. "I changed my mind. It's late."

"No, wait – I'll get rid of him – wait one minute."

"My departure is far from imminent, sir."

"I'll think you'll find your departure is extremely imminent!"

"Yeah, like I said, I'm out of here, you crazy son of a bitch." And with that, Mrs Davenport made a fast exit, slamming the door behind her.

The stranger settled himself into the grey suede armchair nearby, and raised his hand. "Mr Warner," he said, "we don't have many words, so I must entreat you to remain calm, and listen."

"Did you mess up my place like this?"

The man shrugged. "*Mea culpa.*"

"What's that smell?"

The man didn't answer him, but stared outside at the darkening mass of Stanley Park. "How can you bear having so many people under you, and on top of you?"

"What?"

"Never mind. Look – how about a glass of that champagne the lady left without?"

"Forget it."

"An ale, then? I can't leave until I'm permitted to elucidate."

Grudgingly, Jason brought back two beers from the fridge. The man looked in bewilderment at the can, then copied Jason as he cracked his open.

"Right, you have two minutes. First of all – who are you?"

The man got up again, and bowed once more. "I am, sir – your *inspiration.*"

"My what?"

Engrossed in his first sip of beer, the man didn't reply at once. "It's cold – but after all this time, I'm willing to endure it."

"You were about to explain yourself."

"Quite. Mr Warner, could we please be seated. What I have to tell you may come as a shock."

"I prefer to stand."

"Very well." The man sat back down, attempted to sip his beer. "Damn this confounded contraption."

"You were saying."

The man sighed. "Yes. You and me – can't you see the likeness?" He turned his head this way and that. Making himself look, Jason couldn't deny a certain resemblance – in the square cut of the jaw, the colouring, the dark eyes...

"Are you saying we are related?"

"Not exactly. Perhaps, in the future. Look, have you ever read a nineteenth-century English novel called *Sense and Sensibility?*"

"No I have not."

"Well, although it was written a long time ago, you'd find a kindred spirit – no, more like a long-lost brother – in its pages."

"Go on."

"Yes. You both like money, sport, speed, and women – and plenty of them. You are both what they once called a rake. You are both – so I'm told although I can't agree entirely – rather selfish, inconsiderate, and not particularly intelligent. Oh, and uncommonly handsome – let's not forget that."

"Don't tell me. It's you?"

The man bowed low. "Mr John Willoughby at your service – but you may call me *Willoughby*."

"But if you are a fictional character, how can you be sitting here in my apartment, drinking my beer?"

Willoughby hesitated. "Because you're one too."

"What nonsense."

"Didn't you feel my presence, today, Mr Warner, nudging you out of your knavery? Don't you find it odd that the lady neither sees, hears... nor *smells* me... and yet you do?"

Jason sat down now, his mind clambering over potential scenarios for this bizarre claim: he was on *Candid Camera*, Diane Davenport had spiked his drinks, it was some kind of set up, a weird prank...

He slugged at his beer. "Let me get this straight. You're telling me that I'm not real, but am a character in a novel."

Willoughby shook his head. "Not quite. You're in a short story – I'm afraid you're not complex or interesting enough to be the main character in a *novel.*"

"Thanks. So... who's my author?"

"I don't know. A woman, I suspect. An unknown, with a somewhat warped sensibility, if you ask me. *My* creator is Jane Austen, you know... you must have heard of *her.*" His chest puffed up. "I can't say I like the woman – but she's quite the celebrity nowadays, isn't she? Anyway, back to you." He leaned towards Jason, lowered his voice. "I must warn you, Mr Warner, that due to your perpetually incorrigible nature, your author plans to end this story... with your sudden death."

"What absolute crap you talk!" Jason laughed. "I am real – look!" He pulled up his shirt, punched himself in the gut... and carefully cut his finger open on the sharp edge of the beer can. "I feel pain! I exist!"

"What a mess you are making, sir, on your fine white rug. There is no need for such histrionics. Everyone has a creator of some kind, after all. For most, I suppose, it's God himself. For others, it's writers or playwrights or poets. You can still interact with others in your world, after this story ends. But – and here's the rub – once she's done with you, *you cannot change*. Heed my warning on this. I lived only a few years after I married for money; I didn't die "of a broken heart" – but of a most unseemly ailment brought on by my – well, my need for intimacy, let's say. I've been in character purgatory ever since, detained in an odious kind of *pig pen*, can you believe, with nobody to talk to and nothing to do but think about my blockhead existence and wait for my chance at redemption."

"So what happens once you're redeemed?"

Willoughby sighed. "I've no idea. But it's surely preferable to the pig pen. It's all I can manage to keep my cravat clean, and not to stink. My being called here is an excellent start – and I owe that to you. So Jason, mark my words. Choose to change – for both our sakes."

"I've had enough of this nonsense," Jason said, shivering now from a sudden blast of cold night air. "Did you open that window?"

"Oh dear," said Willoughby.

Next thing Jason knew, he was hanging outside his living room window, the one that looked down on the street twelve floors below. He daren't look down, was trying desperately to hold on to the window sill by his fingers, but his arms burned like he'd been there for hours, and as the rain started, he felt his grip start to slip on the wet sill...

"For God's sake!" he cried out. "I believe you, OK! Help me back in, man!"

Willoughby appeared at the window. "Are you quite sure?"

Back inside, Jason paced up and down the room, rubbing his hands, shaking all over.

"What must I do?"

"Well," said Willoughby. "You only have about two hundred words left." He glanced at the answering machine. "You could start with that peculiar device."

Liz.

"Shall I tell you who she is?"

Jason sighed. "Go on."

"She's the direct descendant of one Miss Williams – and a thoughtless knave called Willoughby. You would be doing me a great honour to be kind – where I was not."

Nothing surprised Jason now. "She's related to *you?* But it's not a question of kindness. I like Liz – a lot."

"Is that all? You *like her a lot?*"

"More than anyone I've ever met."

"Except yourself."

"Look," Jason said. "I have been a *rake*, and self-centred, I admit it." Jason glanced back to the window, shut for the time being. "I don't know why. It doesn't make me particularly happy. And I do want to change for the better, really I do... I don't want to die tonight or end up in a pig pen... how much longer do I have?"

"About thirty words."

"OK. Any other advice before you go?"

"Yes. Never let a woman believe you love her, unless you *mean* it. And if you mean it, then always *act* like it."

"Got it," Jason said, reaching for the phone. "Oh, and Willoughby?"

"Yes?"

"Thanks for saving my life."

"Let us hope it proves worthwhile," Willoughby said – and returned to his beer.

❧

My inspiration: With the timeless traits of the rake in mind, I wanted to explore the idea of alternative realities and of interesting leakage between them. Willoughby is the kind of man that women love to love – and then hate – and it's quite easy to visualise a modern version of him, living right here in Vancouver. There are quite of few of them about! I'm aware this piece plays more to the intellect than the emotions, but wanted to see if I could create a readable story from a surreal idea...

A MOST DESIRABLE
CONNECTION

Jasmina Svenne

A Most Desirable Connection

※

Jasmina Svenne

There could be no doubt in any discerning person's mind that the Westfield Ball would prove a great success. Even Lady Belmont said so and *that* Mrs Sidgewick took as the highest compliment.

It had not been easy to reach this point. But all the preparations, both within the kitchen and beyond, paled into insignificance when compared to the difficulty of persuading her firstborn son that there was no escaping his duty.

"You *must* open the ball with Miss Belmont," Mrs Sidgewick had insisted, her heart fluttering in her throat. "She will certainly expect it. You cannot possibly allow that any other unmarried lady can take precedence over her."

"Well, well, Mamma, I will allow that Miss Belmont takes precedence over every other lady in these three parishes," Tom had replied amiably enough and then quite spoilt the effect by adding, "but is it absolutely necessary that *I* should be the one to share her elevation?"

"Of course you must be the one to dance with her. Anything else would be unthinkable. Everyone will expect it. Lady Belmont will expect it."

Mrs Sidgewick could hardly speak rapidly enough in her agitation.

"Oh well, if *Lady Belmont* expects it, she must not be disappointed," Tom replied with a shrug and made his excuses before his mother had quite made up her mind whether his words were sarcastic or not.

Children were a worry, she had confided in Lady Belmont more than once. For some reason she had assumed they would be easier to manage as they grew older, but if that was generally the rule, Tom was most certainly an exception.

Only last autumn he had seemed amenable enough to her suggestions that he should offer Miss Belmont his arm when they were out walking, dance with her at the local Assembly, deliver messages to Belmont Hall and baskets of apples from a particularly fine tree in the Westfield orchard.

It was that last London Season that had quite spoilt him, Mrs Sidgewick thought with a sigh. He had acquired a new wardrobe and a new swagger that she had thought suited him admirably. But there was also something about him now that seemed – well, oddly like rebelliousness. He no longer seemed as biddable as he had been before his absence.

And this was absolutely their last opportunity. If Lady Belmont did take her only child to London next winter – because it was true she *ought* to come out – well, then the Sidgewicks might well have to bid farewell to all hopes of allying themselves with the grandest family in the neighbourhood. The Belmont heiress was sure to have her head turned by some fortune-hunter and then all of Mrs Sidgewick's careful schemes would be at an end.

It was not just the glory of the connection, nor even the extent of Miss Belmont's fortune which, as Mrs Sidgewick was well aware, were above Tom's expectations. To be sure, to have Tom the master of Belmont Hall with an income of ten thousand pounds a year would make things much simpler in the Sidgewick household. She knew that Tom, despite his teasing, was fond of his assorted brothers and sisters and would do something handsome for them if he could.

But the connection was in every way desirable. And the worst of it was, she could not say anything to Tom because then most certainly he would take against the idea. Boys were such contrary creatures, even those who had been taller than their mother by a good head for more years than she cared to count.

To his credit, Tom had done his duty in the end. Mrs Sidgewick had felt as if she had hardly dared breathe until her ear caught the words she had been longing to hear.

"Miss Belmont, will you do me the honour of dancing the first dance with me?"

She had wanted to dance a jig herself and clap her hands and the only thing that restrained her was that Lady Belmont had been talking to her for the past five minutes and, most uncharacteristically, she had not heard a single word. Fortunately her ladyship was a determined-enough talker not to require much more encouragement than the occasional "Very true, my lady", or "Oh, I could not have phrased it better myself", or "I am quite of your opinion".

But now that matters were settled between Tom and Miss Belmont, or at least as far as they could be, Mrs Sidgewick was quite at liberty to attend to Lady Belmont whenever her duties as hostess permitted. It was a nuisance, to be sure, that the Bradburys had been delayed – surely they would have sent their excuses if they were unable to attend? – but it would not take long to greet them and the distant cousin they had begged to be allowed to bring with them, and then the rest of the evening was her own.

Even as the thought crossed her mind, she caught the faint rattle of a carriage on the gravel sweep. A moment later, the ballroom door was opened one last time and the delayed party ushered inside.

"So sorry…shocking state of the roads… the notion of a turnpike trust *must* be mooted again… if Mr Sidgewick and Sir George Belmont were to take the lead, all the others would follow… may I present my cousin, Miss Moreton?"

Miss Moreton proved to be a handsome girl, with the bright eyes and clear complexion of youth and good health. Nay, Mrs Sidgewick, who was in a charitable mood, would even allow that many men might regard her as a very pretty girl.

She could not help being slightly less pleased with Miss Moreton's manners. To be sure, she smiled and replied graciously, but still there was the impression that her eyes kept drifting towards the centre of the room. Though, to be fair, the girl always checked herself if she glanced away for too long.

"So good of you to permit me to come," she murmured, curtseying and inclining her head.

"Oh, think nothing of it," Mrs Sidgewick replied. "We must be sure to introduce you to some of the young people. Though I fear it may be difficult to find you a partner for the first dance. You know what young men are."

"Indeed."

It was possible that Miss Moreton said something more, but if so, Mrs Sidgewick did not hear a word. Her eyes were irresistibly drawn to her oldest son. He had been conversing politely with Miss Belmont, but now he turned his head and instantly changed countenance. In all the twenty-five years she had known him, Mrs Sidgewick had never seen him look so thunderstruck, not even when his younger brother Frank had been obliged to confess that he had entangled Tom's favourite kite in the highest branches of the most venerable oak in Westfield Park.

Whipping her head around to discover the cause of her son's consternation, Mrs Sidgewick was just in time to see a radiant smile illuminate Miss Moreton's face before it wavered.

"M-Miss M-Moreton, I did not expect…" Tom stammered.

The smile sprang back into her eyes.

"Oh, you have not forgotten me, then," she said. "I wasn't sure when my cousins said we were to attend this ball whether it would prove to be the same family…"

"You are acquainted?" Mrs Sidgewick was a little surprised at the shrillness of her voice, but she had caught sight of Miss Belmont's expression, the hardening of her lips, the narrowing of her eyes. The look of a child denied a toy or sugarplum.

"We were introduced to one another in London last year," Tom replied in a tone not quite his own.

Again the smile wavered on Miss Moreton's face. Her lips quivered, as if she was inclined to contradict or amend his bland statement.

"How charming," Mrs Sidgewick intervened hastily. "Now, Tom, is it not time that the dancing commenced? And I must find a partner for Miss Moreton, though to be sure, it will be no easy task. So few gentlemen will exert themselves in the ballroom…"

She had scarce allowed herself to draw breath between sentences before Tom had led Miss Belmont to the top of the room, though not without a backward glance. By the time the longways set had formed, she had safely palmed off Miss Moreton with the youngest Mr Tomlinson, who was admittedly a very poor dancer utterly incapable of remembering the figures of the simplest dance, but who at least was willing to make a fool of himself with a good deal of amiability.

That done, Mrs Sidgewick needed a moment to catch her breath and still the fluttering of her heart before she sought out Mrs Bradbury as the most likely fount of information about Miss Moreton.

What she discovered was not encouraging. Miss Elizabeth

Moreton, as she was properly styled, was the second or third of a number of daughters from her deceased father's second marriage. What little wealth there was in the family had, apparently, been inherited by her older half-brother.

It did not ease Mrs Sidgewick's mind when, as she glanced towards the dancers, she discovered Tom in the process of crossing corners with Miss Moreton. She caught a glimpse of the longing in her son's eyes just as the pair changed places before backing away from each other. She saw Miss Moreton gaze fractionally too long at Tom before taking hands with her partner and Miss Belmont to form a circle.

A few bars more and they would go their separate ways, Tom progressing down the set with Miss Belmont, Miss Moreton and Mr Robert Tomlinson advancing up a place. All might still be well. There was nothing to fret about. Only a few fugitive glances, a few stray words. No more. And yet the unease would not release her.

If Tom were to throw over Miss Belmont in preference for this pretty little nobody, what would become of all her plans for the welfare of her children?

If she had known, if she could have guessed that such an eventuality might happen, she would never have invited the Bradburys. Or maybe if that was not quite consistent with the rules of politeness and hospitality, well then at least she would have urged Tom to engage himself for every dance before Miss Moreton's belated arrival.

But it had been difficult enough persuading Tom to dance with Miss Belmont. She had not wished to raise his hackles by interfering too much. Well, that was what came of being a lenient parent. Her mother had warned her it would do her no good, but she had not heeded her advice.

And so she was forced to watch in helpless agony when, as soon as the first two dances were over and Miss Belmont had been escorted to her seat, Tom made instantly for Miss Moreton.

"So kind of your son to take so much trouble with my cousin, when she does not know a soul here," Mrs Bradbury remarked.

"What? Oh, yes, yes. Tom is… most conscientious about such matters," Mrs Sidgewick murmured distractedly, though Tom had never done anything remotely similar in his life, as far as his mother could recall. She could not help thinking wistfully about the custom of her youth, when she had spent whole evenings dancing with no more than two partners, one for her minuet and another for the country dances.

It seemed, however, that Tom was determined to revive the old custom. Once his initial dances with Miss Moreton were over, he showed no eagerness to leave her or engage another partner. He even seemed aggrieved when obliged to introduce Miss Moreton to other gentlemen.

Such marked partiality for dancing again and again with the same partner could not go unnoticed. More than once, Mrs Sidgewick was on the verge of intervening, but each time, her duties as a hostess obliged her to turn her attention elsewhere.

Fortunately the Bradburys were amongst the first to leave, having one of the longest journeys home. It was only then that Mrs Sidgewick could snatch a moment alone with her son.

He had been leaning against the wall, his arms crossed on his breast, apparently lost in thought as he contemplated the tips of his shoes.

"You're not dancing, Tom?' his mother asked, her tone not quite as bright and brisk as she had intended it to be.

He mustered a pallid smile.

"It would seem not."

"Oh, I am sure there are plenty of young ladies who would

be glad to stand up with you," she rattled away breathlessly as she ran her eyes around the length and width of the room. She barely suppressed a cry of dismay. "Look, Miss Belmont is sitting out. Don't you think it would be a kindness to…"

"Mamma," Tom cut her short, "I know you have only my best interests at heart and I have done my best to please you, but—"

"No, no, don't say it. I don't think I could bear it just now." And she fluttered her fan to try to waft away the tears that had begun gathering in her eyes.

"Dear Mamma, I know you would not wish me to do violence to my feelings in such an important matter as matrimony. And Miss Moreton really is an amiable and accomplished lady. I'm sure you would like her immensely if you were to make her acquaintance properly."

The battle was fierce, but short-lived. She brought herself under control within a very few minutes.

"Well, I have no objection to calling upon Mrs Bradbury in a day or two," she replied and if her voice was a little shaky, her son chose to ignore it. Instead he ducked his head to kiss her cheek.

"Perhaps I ought to go and speak to Miss Belmont," he said. "She looks as if she would rather be dancing than talking to her mother."

"Oh no, you must not raise false hopes…" Mrs Sidgewick faltered, but perhaps Tom did not hear her because he was already striding away.

She let him go. She needed to be alone for a moment, to remind herself that her exertions would soon be over. These would almost certainly be the last dances of the night since numbers had already been reduced by the first wave of departures.

She ran her eyes over the longways set, counting the number of couples and purely by chance her gaze came to rest upon her oldest daughter Catherine. It shocked her anew to see how tall and elegant her little girl had grown. Almost of marriageable age. And was that not Admiral Harvey's grandson dancing with her and gazing at her with open admiration?

If memory served, the admiral was rumoured to be worth several thousand pounds and this grandson was his sole heir. A good match for a girl of Catherine's expectations, if it could only be brought about...

My inspiration: My original inspiration was the scene in which Marianne Dashwood accosts Willoughby in London, but the story and Mrs Sidgewick in particular took on lives of their own.

HARRIET AND THE GYPSIES

Andrew Broadfoot

Harriet and the Gypsies

%C

Andrew Broadfoot

The candle flame flickered as she opened and closed the door, her few steps resonating across the painted wagon's softwood boards. The coffin stood open against the far end of the caravan, its sides nailed roughly from new pine, its panels painted with a dragon with skin shed to a man with one hooked finger. Placed around it were burned candle stubs, etched portraits, gaudy jewellery and all the paraphernalia of a great gypsy king. The man inside was dark, even in death, his face sunken and hollowed out. His hair long and plaited with trailing ribbons, his eyes closed in a way that could not be sleep.

"I've never seen you smile like that your entire life," she said, turning her back on him. The candles flickered and blew out as she closed the door firmly behind her and clopped heavily down the trestle steps in wooden shoes.

It was dark outside, but sultry, hardly a breath of air. She brushed down her skirts and held her bonnet against her chest like a religious supplicant, but they were not pious thoughts that occupied her: only an urgency sixteen years in the making.

Her tribe stood silently, expectantly, burning torches flickering glints of light in their hollow eyes.

"He is ready for heaven now, he will not return," she said.

"Tsuritsa Kalderasha, what now?" The old man stepped forward, his eyes slightly lowered.

"Though death is an unwelcome visitor, he comes regardless and woe betide any man, or woman, who meets him with unsettled affairs."

The crowd shuffled, their breath steaming, keen to go about their night's business.

"Aleandro, we leave immediately it is done. There is unfinished business in England." She rubbed her belly, absently patting the letter she held inside her clothing.

The crowd stepped forward, the children almost charging in their excitement. They sloshed paraffin on and around the wagon, setting it alight with their torches, burning the caravan and the body and everything in it until nothing was left but black ash. Then they packed their effects, hitched the horses and left the final resting place of their dead king, without looking back, lest he yearned to return to them once more.

Tsuritsa watched the skies, limiting the trading with local peoples for fear she should lose time, and all the while answering, or avoiding answering, her adopted people's questions about their business so far away.

"The French, the Austro-Hungarians, the Dutch, they want us to settle, they want us to leave, they want us to drown in their seas. War has come and we are the pariahs both sides will purge. Maybe our life in my homeland might be better."

They would look into her blue eyes, gawping at their own skin like oiled wood and hers like blushing bone and wonder from what world she had descended. But even on a two-month long trek across Europe there was little time for contemplation. The carts constantly broke wheels. The horses needed rested. The children needed to be watched and schooled, food needed finding. Local people were avoided, appeased, defended against. The war, though, was a great and terrible thing; it brought so much wickedness she thought she was in hell.

One night they camped by a snaking river in knotted and rooted ground. They could see the campfires of soldiers, understood their rough French concerned with getting home to deserted farms and well-washed wives, and kept away.

When all were asleep, she pulled out the letter to read in the candlelight.

At that moment, there came a great anguished cry from outside and troopers burst into the encampment, slashing back and forth with swords and swearing loudly in English. Their faces were black with dirt and blood and their eyes glassy with the blood-lust of warriors. One soldier dragged a young woman from her cart, reaching violently inside her clothing. Tsuritsa charged at him, shouting:

"How dare you attack my people, go now or I'll skin your hide from your back and nail you to a hornet tree." She stabbed the man through the shoulder with her brooch-pin and he wheeled round, shrieking insanely. She stopped dead in shock. Not at his language, but at his eyes. They looked back at her with the watery grey rage she had only ever seen in her own husband. But this was not her husband.

"Captain, watch out!" The cry came too late, the French trooper's shot pierced the young captain's tunic and a bloom of blood seeped from within. The light went from his eyes without his ever recognising her.

The gypsies watched the slaughter impassively, waiting only for it to be over. When the French left, taking the dead and captured with them, they set off once more.

Finally, after almost having been driven into the sea along with kinfolk attempting to escape to a new life in the New World, they landed in England and set camp in the woods where they felt safe.

The Gypsy King had bought her and named her Tsuritsa. He said it meant "Light of Dawn" because of her pale skin and fair hair blushed with red.

"You are not my husband," she protested.

"If I am not then who is?" he said, gently.

She hung her head by way of answering him. "Am I to be nothing but a slave to men, a commodity to pass from one to the other?"

"But my lady, you bore another man's child. Did you think your husband would make a happy cuckold? When I came to his door, to sell our jewellery, he ordered us beaten with riding crops, but then he said, 'I will trade,' and that was that. I took you away with me, a sobbing, sorrowful bundle of skirts."

Her slaver that called himself *husband* spoke gently to her, while his people stared bewildered at her alien skin. Her society's accomplishments were useless vanities in her new life.

"It is wrong. I am a good Christian woman, whose only sin is to have been driven to find comfort away from a brutal husband, whose love was only vile fumbling in a fog of drink."

"Ah, but Tsuritsa, my tribe says I should marry a good gypsy girl, keep the blood pure, but me I say no to the matchmaker, I say I marry for love. They say she is not pure, look she has the raw marks of motherhood. I say she will carry my babies and they will be our tribe and you will be happy because I will be happy.

"Where is my baby?"

"I do not know and we do not return to England. I have promised and my oath carries the weight of my bond to my people.

"But she is mine and he took her from me."

"That is a great evil and he will reckon for it, but we set not one foot back in England while I live. What do you want with a man who would sell his own wife? No, you are better with a king who will love you and be faithful, always."

He took her from the country she knew, and the wealth to which she was accustomed. He took her to hot summer lands where she learned of the great Vlad of the Order of the Dragon and of heroic struggles against the forces of the Ottoman Empire. There she learned that her England was but one place among many and that her new people loved her and she them. She had two sons to her new husband, Nikolai and Simenon and she adored them even though they looked nothing like her, with eyes like wet stones and the skins of Moorish princes. But always she thought of her daughter, waiting for the time she might see her. She wrote many letters over the years – her husband permitted her that– but she never received a reply.

The gypsy camp was an untidy affair, strewn between elms and a wide strip of greensward on the outskirts of a small village containing nothing but a handful of houses, a large estate and a munitions arsenal. They did not arrange their various carts, horses, livestock or possessions in any particular order or shape, but rather scattered in family groups each according to their notions or preference, digging their own latrines within the woods.

After their long slog across Europe, stocks were low and they were in dire need of money to buy yarn and cloth and vegetables. It would be months before they could grow their own. The tribe spent the next few weeks exploring the countryside, selling pegs and tablecloths and handkerchiefs and hand-whittled toys, avoiding conflict and waiting. Interminably, waiting.

One hot day, when great puffy clouds scudded across the sky making her pine for the Carpathian Mountains, she made her way down to a well-kempt farm in the valley. There was nothing unusual about the farm, just the usual rooting of pigs in the ground, cattle scattered singly across the field. A young man of twenty-something years watched her arrival, his face a picture of puzzlement. She was overladen with goods and dropped some on the ground. He stepped forward and picked up the peg dolls and examined them.

"I'm afraid you may not find much interest here – in your toys, I mean." She was used to strange behaviour from people, all gypsies were, but this man could not take his eyes off her. "We are all a little old for toys, that's what I mean."

"Maybe you have some washing?"

"Er, pardon me, no, but you… well, you seem so familiar. Are you from around here?"

"Familiar, I doubt that, I have not set foot in England for sixteen years."

The farmer seemed somewhat perplexed, his recalcitrant nature at odds with the questions in his mind.

"You… I mean, it's your skin and your eyes, you don't look like any gypsy I've ever seen. And, if you don't mind my saying so, your accent is English, Somerset even, or somewhere to the west."

Her arms were tired and, much as she was used to walking, she needed to take the weight off her feet.

"Would you mind if I had a drink of water, perhaps I might sit for a short while?" She watched him walk back into the house and considered what she might say next. Who was it he saw in her? "Thank you most kindly," she said, sipping delicately from the glass as if she had travelled decades into the past. "Young man, you asked if I had family here, what did you mean?"

He gazed at her for a while as he could divine some truth from behind her eyes.

"It is nothing, but you have the look of a local girl of my acquaintance…"

Is he blushing?

"Well, she is quite the fairest… There is something in your eyes, it reminded me of her."

Much refreshed and anxious not to stay longer than necessary without a trade, she made to leave.

"You have been very kind –"

"Perhaps I might take a couple of these dollies, perhaps, in the not too distant future I might…"

"Maybe this young lady might be a little closer to you than an 'acquaintance'?"

"I certainly hope so. You may see her. On occasion she walks the road near your encampment…" Then his shyness overtook him again. In all, Tsuritsa succeeded in relieving herself of some half of her toys and sewn cottons, and made a much brighter journey home.

The following day she sat in front of the camp and watched the road for a young woman she might recognise. Once settled, sure she would not be interrupted she read the crumpled letter once more:

My dearest Lady,

I write to you with not a little trepidation, for I fear that my own preoccupations with romance and intrigue have led me to make the direst errors of judgement. What is more, I have no way of knowing whether in informing you I have unearthed a truth and relieved you of a great burden, or whether I am opening Pandora's Box and destroying the settled lives of good people. I must admit myself to having an interest as I have succeeded in marrying the kindest and noblest of men, whose peace will be most horribly shattered, but I cannot, yet, find it within myself to inform him of my discoveries. However, madam, I believe you have suffered the direst of wrongs and I believe I must tell you what I know.

Some few years ago, when (much under the influence of Ann Radcliffe) investigating the contents of an old trunk I came across papers, household bills, laundry lists and so on. Interrupted by the sternest of maids and in panic I secreted the papers about my person. Suddenly evicted in a shameful manner from that house (I am quite sure you will understand, fully!) I placed them in an out-of-the-way drawer within my own home, quite convinced they were of no importance. It was not until I was married and living at the vicarage that I came across the papers and discovered your letters within them. So horrified was I and so determined to find the truth, that I made some enquiries. I believe, Mrs Tilney, that I have found your daughter living with kindly folks in the village of Highbury.

Please do with this information what your conscience will,
Your faithful daughter-in-law
Catherine Tilney

Tsuritsa heard unfamiliar giggling and saw the two young women almost skipping along the road. Hastening to the camp she spoke to a stout middle-aged woman.

"Jofranke, take the children, Ellie, Emerald, some others and ask those ladies if they might like to see some of the jewellery we make. Don't take no for an answer."

Jofranke and the gypsy children took off after them dancing excitedly, talking in their mixed-up English, tugging at their skirts.

"Lady, you come see beautiful things."

The young women seemed suddenly flustered.

"Go away, please, we've got no more money."

"No, not money, we show you?"

However, it was no use; one of the women was already running away like no English girl does. Tsuritsa stepped out and studied the visceral and unfathomable fear her daughter had for her own mother's people and watched sadly as a man came charging on horseback, scattering the children with great force and hurry and scooping her away. The figures receded into the distance across the field. She cooed over the children, concerned they were hurt, but they only laughed at the craziness of the English.

"Come," Tsuritsa said. "Our business in England is concluded." Then she bundled her belongings into her cart and took her tribe with her...

❦

My inspiration: What if the gypsies in *Emma* had a greater purpose than mischief and Harriet's past not so easily explained away? What if *Northanger Abbey* did have a dark secret..?

JANE AUSTEN, 1945

Elisabeth Lenckos

Jane Austen, 1945

⁊ℭ

Elisabeth Lenckos

What a lovely book to come out of the rubble. Small and soft, it fits beautifully into my hand. I caress its leather covers (once green, I think), from which the gilt edging has almost rubbed off. I feel the pages, which are frayed and stained by mud, or is it blood? Yet this was a Christmas gift.

Or so went the story...

Men are at play in a field. It is a sodden field, foul. They are wearing military uniforms, English and German, but their weapons are strewn on the ground, unused, at least for now. For once, theirs is not a game to the death; they are kicking a football. It is Christmas, so eventually presents change hands. Nothing is new; the men give what they have carried with them from home. My father hands over his signet ring. The Englishman opposite him offers him a small, green book. My father reads the words *Pride and Prejudice*. He translates them slowly into his native language, *Stolz und Vorurteil*. He smiles. The Englishman nods, "This is a story about the British when they were at their best. Not what we are like, here, now; animals in trenches. Yes, there was suffering, but not like this. Not for us, at least..."

Or, not a gift at all, but a spoil of war...

The truce does not last. Yet another day of fighting; the English are going over the top, the Germans accompany the dances of death with the bellowing of their machine guns. A Tommy is shot in the heart. He goes down by a Jerry trench and perishes in agony. My father is sent out to search his body after dark. He does so, trembling with fear and distress. But then, he finds a small, green book in the dead man's jacket pocket. My father translates the title, *Stolz und Vorurteil*. He smiles. He read this book as a student. He tries to wipe off the blood, but the stains have dried by now. He hides this treasure in his jacket pocket, precious to my father because it reminds him of what it was like before the slaughter began. My father admired the English, since, as he saw it, they had no tyrants; but instead, a society of gentlemen and gentlewomen, great houses, and fine libraries. English tailors were to him the best in the world. Jermyn (German?) Street. Oxford. Bath. London. London!

Against all odds, my father survived his first war. He saved the symbol of his one-sided love affair and passed it on to me. Before I could understand English, he purchased a German translation. When I learned English, he read to me from the small, green book. Thus, I owe my love of Jane Austen to a chance encounter between two men, mortal enemies, exchanging such objects as they happened to have on them during one memorable Christmas in 1914. Or, I owe it to my father's robbing an Englishman's corpse of its one precious possession, a copy of *Pride and Prejudice*, one fateful night. Take your pick. Only don't judge.

But this was not the end of the story for the small, green book. In 1945, I held the Englishman's gift in my hands again, after I had gone through what remained of our firebombed home. The descendants of the soldier, assuming that my father had thieved *Pride and Prejudice* from him after all, had visited my city as avenging angels. Berlin was in ruins. My mother and I were relieved; the reign of terror was over.

Yet, we also mourned. For in the meantime, I had lost my virginity, and I was only thirteen. But I was alive, and that was something. In fact, I had risen from the dead, in a sense; and with the help of Mr Darcy.

The year before, my mother had dug a hole for me the size of my body. She had done so to keep me safe from the Russian soldiers ravaging the women of Berlin. After she had placed me in this hole, she had covered me with earth, leaving small openings only for my nose and mouth. She begged me to remain where I was until she returned a few hours later. I did as she said. There I lay, protected from harm, until she came back to release me. But the time in my makeshift burrow passed slowly. My bones grew colder and damper; I breathed uneasily through the clumps of mud heaped upon me. The hardest thing was to keep still. My legs and arms were cramping and hurting all the while.

This was the moment when I first began to take my mind elsewhere; to the evenings when my father read to me from *Pride and Prejudice*. He had left the novel on my bedside table when he had gone to his second war a year earlier, despite the asthma that had been another legacy of the first war he had fought. I heard his voice again, telling me of the time when Mr Darcy and Mr Bingley moved into Netherfield and, warmed by the autumn sun, walked, danced, and flirted with Elizabeth and Jane Bennet. I reprised my favorite scenes from the book, turning the words into beautiful images in which I lost myself. It helped pass the time in that ditch, truly it did.

I should explain that the bolt hole my mother made for me was not in the inner city, but the far northern outskirts of Berlin. Here she and I had fled, with our dog Gertie, in a panic, during the last days of the war. My parents owned a little dacha in the village of Lehnitz which, as it turned out, lay right in the path of the advancing Russian forces. During the first days of the occupation my mother was able to take me into the garden behind the dacha and bury me before the soldiers came looking for women and blood. But nemesis was lying in wait for us.

That my mother had been able to take me to my hiding place in time we owed to our Gertie, an Airedale Terrier, who possessed an acute ability to sense peril. She whined at the slightest alteration in the atmosphere, even when it occurred miles away. (Just where had my mother got a hold of an English breed in wartime Berlin? This might make another interesting story.) In the past, she had alerted us to Nazi death squads and roving gangs. One of them had shot off her left ear, making her partially deaf. Perhaps that was why on one particular day she was not aware of the approaching Russian soldier who was about to claim our dacha and its women as his own. He had caught up with her before she could warn my mother and me, and he had silenced her quickly.

The Russian entered the cottage just as we were about to sit down to our wartime dinner, potato peel soup, in the front room. I was tall for my age, and he sized me up quickly. He signaled to my mother to retreat to the kitchen in the back and to close the door. Without much ceremony, he took me on the floor. Afterwards, he called for my mother to return, asking that the two of us sit down and eat with him. Then he locked me in the kitchen, for now it was my mother's turn. This went on for many days, during which the Russian became a regular visitor. Sometimes, he brought us food. He took things from us, too: my mother's jewellery, my father's watch – his books we had left in the city. 'Our Russian', as we came to call him, was not too cruel; we knew this because we had seen the mutilated corpses of neighboring women when we ventured outside. My mother said, too late, that we should have remained in Berlin since the part of the city where we lived was rumored to have been placed under British protection.

After I was raped for the third time, I lay on the floor of our dacha, and sleep would not come. This was the moment when I understood that I needed more than visions of beauty to keep the horror at bay. Searching for a mental exercise that would prevent my brain from slipping sideways into the void of despair, I had a sudden inspiration: I would 'mind-read,' that is, read a book from memory. Again, I chose *Pride and Prejudice*. I travelled, in thought, from this dreadful place where I had just been with a man who did not love me, to the sites in the story my father had lovingly shared with me, first in my own, then in Austen's language.

Of course, my mind-reading was no orderly process, but I tried to make it so. I did not begin with 'It is a truth universally acknowledged,' but with my favorite scene, the ball at Meryton. The night when Mr Darcy wounds Elizabeth Bennet's pride by refusing to dance with her, she exerts her revenge by ridiculing his arrogance, and he falls in love with her because of the intelligent sparkle he sees in her eyes. Or that is the way I remembered it. I enjoyed envisioning the encounter between them; I had done so already in my dugout. But that night I attempted to recollect the words Mr Darcy and Elizabeth spoke to one another, the language with which Austen described their strong, clashing personalities, and the subtle ways in which she intimated their mutual, unacknowledged attraction.

The Meryton ball was not too difficult to recall, but I ran into trouble when I wanted to move on to the scenes that followed. The harder I tried, the more the exact plot eluded me. It had been too long since my father had last read *Pride and Prejudice* to me. I confused sequences of events and omitted important details. At, times I was unable to make the plot cohere. Soon, I began to get frustrated. But then, I had another idea: I pretended that I was the director of an amateur theatrical, selecting the scenes from the novel I wanted to stage. I concentrated on one scene at a time. I assembled the principal players; then I added the lesser characters. I outlined the setting and the action and finally, I went about recreating the dialogue. This make-believe task proved effective. I became immersed into the world of my imaginary drama. Eventually, I fell asleep. Whenever I woke in the night, I would go back to my work.

Reading Jane Austen in my mind became my nocturnal pastime after the Russian left; adapting *Pride and Prejudice* for my theatre of thought turned into my nightly consolation. It made me determined to go on living, despite what was being done to me. I had to find out how the book ended. During my retrieval of the story, I used Mr Darcy as my guide. (I don't know why I chose a man's perspective. Was it to think myself into the male psyche, or to remind myself that a man could both change and be kind?) I asked: Why did he reject Elizabeth at first? How did he cope with the surprise of his unexpected fall into love? What were the words he used to describe his conflicting emotions when he first proposed to her? What was in that letter, again? Answering these questions kept me sane. The lovely, rational world into which I vanished each night was the opposite of the brutality and destruction I encountered during the day. *Pride and Prejudice* gave me the strength to cope.

My reading also made me realise the importance Austen's characters placed on observation and on conversation. I started to watch my captor and to talk to him, although he knew only a few words of German. But no matter, I had noticed that he was quite sentimental; he often cried after he violated me. In this act, I saw my chance for survival. I communicated to him that I shared his sorrow, so that he would begin to see me as a human being. It took some time, but it worked. I am convinced now that it saved my mother's and my life. 'Our Russian' bonded with us, so when the time came for him to move on, he allowed us to live. Many of his comrades did not show such mercy. I know that we were fortunate to make it through the Russian occupation at all. But I also believe that we survived because I learned from Austen: she taught me how to decode people and to relate to them.

Most of all, reading Austen allowed me to persevere. Each night, I reminded myself that life could be as beautiful as *Pride and Prejudice*, and that for every Wickham, there is a Darcy. I wanted to grow into a woman and to meet such a man. And this is what happened, years later. But before, in 1945, my mother and I were simply glad to be permitted to return to our neighborhood in the British sector of Berlin. Our apartment had been destroyed, but as I sorted through its debris, I found the small, green book 'by a lady', which I still own. My father was to die of starvation in a Russian prisoner-of-war camp, but I lived. I studied English and made myself fluent in the language of the author who saved my life. I married...

After the war, when I could not make myself read German literature because it seemed tainted by the dreadful history I had witnessed, Austen's book sustained me, as it had my father. Yes, I knew by then that the English soldier my father met during the wartime football game had not been entirely correct in what he said. Regency England was no stranger to carnage and pain; of course not. But when Germany was vile, England, by way of the soldier, was good to my father, and through him, to me: it gave us Jane Austen.

My father read Austen after returning from the trenches of the First World War. I 'read' Austen trying to survive under the ruthless regime that had been created in the wake of that calamity: *Pride and Prejudice* made us both take heart. For this gift, I am indebted to the English soldier, who passed the small, green book on to my father. As I come to the end of my life, I believe that he did so in the way my father told the story first, before the madness set in. Wittingly, one Christmas in 1914, a man gave another man a reason to carry on: reading, believing.

Jane Austen, 1945

❧

My inspiration: This story was inspired by the wartime stories of my grandmother and mother, as well as our shared love of Jane Austen and English literature. I dedicate 'Jane Austen, 1945' to the muses at Chawton House Library. They supported my work with a generous fellowship that enabled me to spend time with my favorite British author in 2009 and 2010, and they have done me the favour of taking an interest in this short story, which is my first. Thank you for your personal kindness and professional munificence.

Biographies

Sarah Barr read English at London University and now teaches creative writing in Dorset, where she lives, and for the Open University. She likes writing on trains and buses, in cafes and gardens – wherever she can find some inspiration and time. She tends to write about relationships, including our relationship with the natural world. She enjoyed re-visiting Lyme Regis for the setting of her Jane Austen story. Her short stories and poems have been published in various magazines and anthologies, including, *The Yellow Room, The Bridport Prize Anthology 2010, South, The Lady, The Penniless Press* and *The Interpreter's House.*

Jacqueline Barrios lives, writes and teaches literature in Los Angeles, California. Born in Singapore in 1979, she spent her childhood and adolescence in Malaysia and the Philippines before moving to California. She studied literature and creative writing at University of California at Berkeley, where she also earned her Master's in Education. She is currently working on her Master's in English at University of California at Irvine while developing a theatre workshop for urban high school students that included a full-length, live production of *Pride and Prejudice*. She is working on a collection of short stories inspired by a life lived through, by and for a love for literature.

Holly Dale Bern lives in Mequon, Wisconsin and is a member of the Jane Austen Society of North America. She has an MFA in Writing and Literature from Bennington College, Vermont and a JD degree from Hastings College of Law, San Francisco. She is an inactive member of the California Bar. For composing purposes, Holly finds helpful the words of the poet Robert Frost: *No tears in the writer, no tears in the reader. No surprise in the writer, no surprise in the reader.* She believes this counsel extends nicely to laughter as well. *People of the Book* is her second published story.

Andrew Broadfoot loves to read. His reading is almost as eclectic as his choice of jobs, having been a trawler fisherman, dry stone dyke builder and chef. What fascinates him about Jane Austen is the way she handled serious and comedic elements simultaneously with such a light hand and brought together seemingly disparate elements, weaving them into a satisfactory whole.

This competition gave Andrew the opportunity to splice together stories from two very different novels and explore what happens. The award suggests Andrew's story is readable, which he feels is wholly due to having a tolerant and supportive partner, who is very polite and positive about his abilities.

Paul Brownsey is the winner of the Jane Austen Short Story Award 2011. He left school in 1961 to become a newspaper reporter in Luton and went to university late (Keele, Oxford and Swarthmore College, Pennsylvania). Subsequently he was lecturer in philosophy at Glasgow University until he retired in 2009. His stories have appeared in about 50 magazines and collections in the UK, Ireland and North America. An earlier story inspired by Jane Austen was published in *Staple* in 2004 and is available at http://www.poetrymagazines.org.uk/magazine/record.asp?id=13741

or Google 'Duncarnock Hill Brownsey'. He lives with his civil partner, Jim McKenzie, in Bearsden, north of Glasgow.

Judith Earnshaw was born in 1945, educated at Bedales, Cambridge and London universities. She trained as a psychotherapist, but always worked with offenders. Two adult children working in visual arts regularly say: 'Oh Mum, you're not in Court again!' Hoping for a second career as a writer when she retires at 70 and lets loose the crime novels that are in her blood. She lives within walking distance of Chawton House. Would she have got on with Jane Austen? She thinks so. They share moral ideals and an acid take on life.

Mary Fitzpatrick is one of the two runners-up for the Jane Austen Short Story Award 2011. A graduate of the University of Glasgow, she has taught English Literature to both children and adults but currently works for a charity. Her interest in creative writing was sparked at school by her favourite teacher, Brother Everard, who said he liked her 'compositions'. Recently she completed an Open University creative writing course, which really helped her to focus. She has also attended numerous writing courses, including one run by the Arvon Foundation. Mary lives in rural Scotland and as well as writing she enjoys cycling, walking in the woods spotting red squirrels, cooking and sipping wine.

Elaine Grotefeld was born in Montreal and raised in the UK – long enough ago to have enjoyed first reading *Pride and Prejudice* without knowing anything about it. The handsome, charming Mr Wickham reeled her in too. She read English at Jesus College, Cambridge, too like Lydia Bennet to do it justice apart from one decent dissertation – on Jane Austen. Since then, Elaine has lived and worked in London,

Vancouver, Hong Kong and Singapore. In Asia she 'head-hunted' technology executives by day and wrote stories by night quite a few of which have been published in magazines or anthologies. Now back in Vancouver, Elaine's been busy ignoring her children's needs and completing her novel manuscript. *Meeting Joe McManus* explores what can happen after you meet – and agree to go away with – a man who might just be too good to be true…

Sulaxana Hippisley teaches A-level English literature in a sixth form college in North London. She was introduced to Austen at the age of fifteen by her English teacher. Whilst reading English at university, she became interested in Austen's representations of marriage and class in Regency England and the prevalence of these issues in contemporary Indian and Sri Lankan societies. In addition to sharing her love of Austen with her students, Sulaxana enjoys Indian cinema from the 1950s and 60s and is currently working on a collection of short stories about her mother's upbringing in post-independence Sri Lanka.

Marybeth Ihle, a native New Yorker, began her lifelong love of all things British after reading *The Secret Garden* at a young age. Discovering Jane Austen's novels and Masterpiece Theatre a few years later sealed the deal. Marybeth has a Bachelor's Degree in English Literature from Binghamton University and a Master's in Communications from Georgetown University. She works in New York City and is currently adapting Jane Austen's unfinished manuscript *The Watsons* into a screenplay. She was one of those Americans who woke up at 3.45am to watch the royal wedding. *Persuasion* is her favourite novel.

Rebecca Lees is from Pontypridd in South Wales, working as a communications officer for one half of the week and a freelance journalist and copywriter for the other. Rebecca needs more halves in the week as she has two busy children and a VW camper van called Emily, who all need a lot of attention. Rebecca enjoys rock climbing, camping and walking and is starting to panic about the deadline of a walking trails book she has been commissioned to write. She has previously had short fiction included in Honno's *Cut on the Bias*.

Elisabeth Lenckos is an instructor at the University of Chicago. A Fulbright scholar, she has studied and taught in Germany, England, Spain and the United States. Elisabeth is a translator of Holocaust poetry and currently at work on two books about Jane Austen. She lives with her husband John and her Bearded Collie, Wimsey, in Chicago and Berlin.

Colette O'Connor is a first year literature undergraduate at the University of Glasgow, where she is the president of Student Action for Refugees. While still at school, her award-winning one act play *After Icarus* was performed by the Andrew Cotterel Theatre Company and featured as part of Kingston's International Youth Arts Festival. She enjoys writing free verse poetry and is especially interested in themes of gender and sexuality. This is her first published work.

Susan Piper was born and raised in Canada where she gained a degree in Drama and English. She has also lived in New York, studying acting, and in London. Susan has, for the last 20 years, made her home in Hampshire with her very supportive partner, a tree surgeon, and their two teenage children. She recently left full-time employment as a primary school teacher so she could devote more time to writing and painting. She continues to teach on a 'supply' basis and offers one-to-one tuition as needed by a local school – the children she works with provide constant inspiration! One of her short stories, *As One Door Closes...*, won the Enrico Charles Literary Award at the Winchester Writers' Conference. This award is for fact or fiction that highlights issues surrounding disability.

Rebecca Rouillard was born in Oxford, grew up in South Africa and recently moved back to the UK. She had always planned to be a writer one day. At thirty she decided she had waited quite long enough and enrolled in a creative writing course at Birkbeck College in London. When she's not writing she is a freelance graphic designer. She is married to Paul, long-time patron of the arts, and has two children.

Deirdre Shanahan is one of the two runners-up for the Jane Austen Short Story Award 2011. Her short stories have been published in the USA, Ireland and the UK, including *The Massachusetts Review*, *The Southern Review* and *Iowa Woman*. Her work has also been published in *New Writing* from Vintage, *Well Sorted* from Serpent's Tail, and *The Phoenix Book of Irish Short Stories*. She has been awarded a grant from Arts Council England to work on a novel.

Jasmina Svenne was born in Derby to Latvian parents, but has lived most of her life in Nottinghamshire. Her first novel *Behind the Mask* was published in 2001, but although all 400 copies sold out and she was shortlisted for the RNA's New Writers' Award, her subsequent attempts to sell a second novel have all been unsuccessful.

Meanwhile she has honed her writing skills by writing novella-length historical romances for *My Weekly* Pocket Novels, six of which (so far) are available in large print. She also came second in the 2011 Waterloo Short Story Competition. Her interests include reading, baking and historical dance.

Sarah Todd Taylor moved from Yorkshire to west Wales at the age of eight and now lives in Aberystwyth. Her short stories have featured in several Honno anthologies and she has had a short monologue produced by BBC Radio Five Live. She works in education and, as well as writing, she spends her spare time singing opera.

Jocelyn Watson grew up in Hong Kong with a mixed Indian and English heritage. After qualifying as a lawyer she began writing in 1987 supported by the Asian Women's Writers Collective. In 2001, the Women's Press published her first short story in an anthology called *Long Journey Home*. She has presented her writings at the Haringey Literary Festival, the Libertas Lesbian Book Festival and University of Kent, and went on to do an MA in Creative Writing. She now teaches creative writing to women in Tottenham and is currently working on her first novel.

Les Wood was weaned on Jane Austen in rural Devon and shares her mother's lifelong passion for constant re-reading of her novels. Having single-handedly reared four children to dubious adulthood, health issues have now allowed Les the space to explore her interest in creative writing – although lack of confidence prevents most of her projects actually reaching fruition or completion. *The Darcy Syndrome* is her first successful literary effort but hopefully not her last; she is currently working on her first humorous novel and – with any luck – she may even finish it! She is also an indefatigable Oxfam bookshop and stewarding volunteer.

The Judges

Michèle Roberts is the author of twelve highly acclaimed novels, including *The Looking Glass* and *Daughters of the House*, which won the WH Smith Literary Award and was shortlisted for the Booker Prize. Her memoir *Paper Houses* was BBC Radio 4's Book of the Week in June 2007. She has also published poetry and short stories, most recently collected in *Mud – stories of sex and love* (2010). Half-English and half-French, Michèle Roberts lives in London and in the Mayenne, France. She is Emeritus Professor of Creative Writing at the University of East Anglia.

Lindsay Ashford is a former BBC journalist and the author of six published crime novels. Her second, *Strange Blood*, was shortlisted for the Theakston's Old Peculier Crime Novel of the Year Award. She has had short stories published and broadcast on BBC Radio 4 and has edited two collections of short fiction and prose for Honno: *Written in Blood* and *Strange Days Indeed*. Her latest novel, *The Mysterious Death of Miss Austen* (Honno, 2011), was inspired by working at Chawton House and living in its environs. She splits her time between Hampshire and a home on the Welsh coast.

Janet Thomas is a freelance editor and lives in Aberystwyth. She has edited a wide range of books, including four short story anthologies for Honno: *Catwomen from Hell*, *The Woman Who Loved Cucumbers*, *Mirror, Mirror* and *Safe World Gone*, which were co-edited with Patricia Duncker. She has published short stories and her children's picture book *Can I Play?* (Egmont) won a *Practical Pre-School* gold award.

More from Honno

Dancing with Mr Darcy
The first collection of the
Chawton House Library
Award winning stories
with an introduction
by Sarah Waters. Tales
inspired by the work of
Jane Austen and Chawton
House.
ISBN: 978-1-906784-08-9
£7.99

Founded in 1986 to
publish the best of women's
writing, Honno publishes
a wide range of titles from
Welsh women.

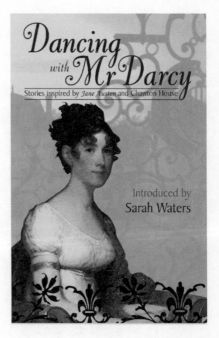

Praise for Honno's books
'a marvellous compilation of reminiscences' _Time Out_
'a cracking good read' dovegreyreader.co.uk
'illuminating, poignant, entertaining and unputdownable'
The Big Issue

All Honno titles can be ordered online at www.honno.co.uk or by
sending a cheque to Honno with free p&p to all UK addresses.